A Note from Stephanie about the Junior High Talent Show

My best friends Darcy and Allie and I would do just about anything to beat the Flamingoes at the talent show. The Flamingoes are this bunch of older girls who think they're really cool. They've outsmarted us before, and this time they even have all the talent show judges on their side. Believe me, things got complicated when one of the judges asked me out on a real date. . . .

But before I tell you more, let me explain my family situation, in case you don't already know.

I come from a *very* large family.

Right now there are nine people and a dog living in our house—and for all I know, someone new could move in at any time. There's me, my big sister, D.J., my little sister, Michelle, and my dad, Danny. But that's just the beginning.

Uncle Jesse came first. My dad asked him to come live with us when my mom died, to help take care of me and my sisters.

Back then, Uncle Jesse didn't know much about taking care of three little girls. He was more into rock 'n' roll. So Dad asked his old college buddy, Joey Gladstone, to help out. Joey didn't know anything about kids, either—but it sure was funny watching him learn!

Having Uncle Jesse and Joey around was like having three dads instead of one! But then something even better happened—Uncle Jesse fell in love. He married Becky Donaldson, Dad's co-host on his TV show, *Wake Up, San Francisco*. Aunt Becky's so nice—she's more like a big sister than an aunt.

Next Uncle Jesse and Aunt Becky had twin baby boys. Their names are Nicky and Alex, and they are adorable!

I love being part of a big family. Still, things can get pretty crazy when you live in such a full house!

FULL HOUSE™: STEPHANIE novels

Phone Call from a Flamingo
The Boy-Oh-Boy Next Door
Twin Troubles
Hip Hop Till You Drop

Available from MINSTREL Books

FULL HOUSE™
Stephanie

Hip Hop Till You Drop

Devra Newberger Speregen

A Parachute Press Book

A MINSTREL® BOOK

PUBLISHED BY POCKET BOOKS

New York   London   Toronto   Sydney   Tokyo   Singapore

A MINSTREL PAPERBACK *ORIGINAL*

 A Minstrel Book published by
POCKET BOOKS, a division of Simon & Schuster Inc.
1230 Avenue of the Americas, New York, NY 10020

A Parachute Press Book
Copyright © 1994 by Lorimar Television, Inc.

FULL HOUSE, characters, names, and all related indicia are trademarks of Lorimar Television © 1994.

ISBN: 0-671-88291-0

First Minstrel Books printing April 1994

10 9 8 7 6 5 4 3 2 1

A MINSTREL BOOK and colophon are registered trademarks of Simon & Schuster Inc.

Printed in the U.S.A.

Hip Hop Till You Drop

CHAPTER
1

◆ ◢ ◣ ◆

"Hey, Ian, tell me the truth," said Stephanie Tanner, looking across the picnic table at something rare: a boy who was also a good friend. Stephanie had known Ian Ezratty, who was a year ahead of her in school, since before she could remember. She trusted him one hundred percent to give her an honest opinion.

Ian, however, had just taken an enormous bite of his hamburger and was unable to tell her anything. All he could do was nod and wave a hand around in front of his mouth.

Stephanie laughed. "Okay, when you swallow, tell me what you think. Is Jenni Morris a really, truly fabulous dancer?"

Ian wrinkled his nose as if something smelled bad.

"You don't think so?" Stephanie said. "Really?"

Ian nodded. And when at last he got the bite down, he took a long swig of his lemonade and said, "Why?"

"Well, you know how Jenni and her Flamingoes bulldozed the eighth graders into making more money than the sixth graders for the big library fund-raising project?"

Ian nodded again.

"Well," said Stephanie, "I think it's time for us sixth graders to get our act together, you know?" She looked thoughtful. "The Flamingoes are entering a dance number in the school talent show. But Allie, Darcy, and I are the best dancers in the sixth grade, and I think we can beat the Flamingoes."

"Such modesty," Ian said.

"Allie and Darcy are coming over so we can practice," said Stephanie. "They should be here pretty soon. If you're lucky, we'll let you watch."

"How can I ever thank you?" Ian said, laughing.

Then Stephanie turned her attention to finishing her hamburger so it would be fully digested by the time she started hip hopping around.

Stephanie's family and the Ezrattys—Ian, his mom, and his dad—often got together for barbecues. Stephanie's dad, Danny Tanner, and Mike and Helene Ezratty had gone to college together. And Joey Gladstone—who lived with the Tanners—had gone with them. They all loved to get together to swap stories about their good old college days. By now Stephanie and the rest of the family knew most of the stories by heart.

"Hey, Mike!" Danny Tanner said as he put three more hot dogs on the grill. "Tell them about that time Joey and I woke you up at eight and told you you were late for your psych final!"

Mike Ezratty opened his mouth to speak, but Joey jumped in to tell the story instead.

"Mike bolts out of bed," Joey explained to everyone. "And throws on his clothes backward and everything because he's still half-asleep!"

"Mike is screaming at everybody," Danny butted in, "hopping around the dorm with his pants on one leg, and he's looking all over for his lucky exam pen. 'I'm late! I'm late! Where's

3

my pen?' he's screaming up and down the halls. Meanwhile, if he had even bothered to look out a window, he would have realized that it was still nighttime! Joey and I had reset his alarm for eight *p.m.* while he was taking a nap. His midterm wasn't for another twelve hours!''

Danny and Joey did a high-five across the picnic table, laughing so hard they could barely catch their breath. After a minute, they realized that they were the only ones laughing.

"What?" Danny asked, his laughter dying down. "Isn't that funny?" He looked around the table.

"Dad," Stephanie said, "it was funny the *first* time you told it. And even the second and third times. But ... you've told that story a hundred times already!"

"Well, Jesse and Rebecca have never heard it," Danny said stiffly. Uncle Jesse and Aunt Becky lived on the top floor of the Tanners' house with their little twin boys.

Everyone looked over to Jesse and Becky. Jesse had his head down on the picnic table.

"I think he's snoring!" Stephanie said, giggling.

Becky gave her husband a little kick.

"Wha?" Jesse said, sitting up quickly. "Oh . . . what a story, Dan! Boy, you were really a little devil back in college, huh?"

"Forget it, Jess," Becky said. "They saw you sleeping."

"I wasn't sleeping," Jesse said. "Would you believe I was, uh, looking for one of my contact lenses?"

"You don't wear contact lenses," seven-year-old Michelle Tanner said.

Jesse shot her a look.

"You don't even wear glasses," Stephanie called out.

"Thanks for pointing that out, guys!" Jesse made a face.

"You're welcome, Uncle Jesse," Michelle said. "I thought your story was funny, Daddy," she added.

Danny looked sweetly at his youngest daughter. "Thank you, Michelle. At least somebody around here has a sense of humor."

"I didn't understand it," Michelle added, "but it was really funny the way you told it!"

That made everybody laugh—even Danny. "Well, it's better than nothing," he said.

"Not better than that Parents' Visiting Day!" Joey exclaimed.

Stephanie and Ian groaned. Jesse put his head back down on the table.

"No, please!" begged D.J., Stephanie's seventeen-year-old sister. "Not that story again!"

"Oh, but this is *really* funny," Joey said.

"Actually," said Danny, "it isn't."

"See," said Joey, starting in, "Danny'd just finished cleaning our dorm room that morning because his parents were coming to visit. He was a neat-freak even back then."

"Hey," Danny interrupted. "Just because you never once picked up a vacuum or a dust rag during the entire four years we lived together . . ." He looked at Joey and shook his head in disgust.

"Anyway," Joey went on, "the room was spotless, and in walks Mike with . . ."

"Two stray, muddy dogs!" Stephanie, D.J., and Ian all yelled out, finishing for him.

"And they ran around the room and turned the place into a muddy mess, just as Grandma and Grandpa walked in," Stephanie finished.

Joey stopped in midlaugh. "Yup, that's what happened," he said. "But you gotta admit . . . it *was* funny."

Stephanie rolled her eyes.

"Dad?" Michelle said. "Can we have dessert now?"

The mention of dessert got a response from everyone. They had all seen the scrumptious-looking chocolate mousse cake Mike and Helene Ezratty had walked in with.

"Sure, Michelle!" Danny said.

Uncle Jesse hopped up from the table. "Good idea, Michelle," he said. "I'll go get the cake."

"No! No!" D.J. said. "Please . . . let me!"

"Me too!" Michelle yelled, running after her sister.

"No, I think I should get it!" Becky said, bolting for the kitchen door.

"Not if I get to it first!" Jesse said, running after her.

Suddenly D.J. turned around. "Hey! Wait a sec. Where are the twins?" she asked frantically. "They were just here."

Jesse and Becky stopped in their tracks and

7

looked around the backyard in a panic. "Where could they be?" Becky cried.

As Jesse and Becky began wildly searching the backyard, D.J. and Michelle sprinted to the door.

"Uncle Jesse! Aunt Becky!" Stephanie called. "You put the twins down for a nap an hour ago, remember?"

"That was really sneaky, D.J.!" Jesse yelled, and he and Becky darted after D.J. and Michelle.

"It's too bad," Danny remarked when they were gone. "They're going to miss one great story!"

"I think they'll get over it, Dad," Stephanie said, laughing. She looked at Ian, and he smiled back at her.

Danny, Joey, Mike, and Helene, sitting on lawn chairs, returned to talking about the good old days. That left Stephanie and Ian alone at the end of the picnic table.

"Have you picked the music you'll dance to at the talent show?" Ian asked.

"Yeah, we found a great En Vogue song. I've figured out most of the steps, and I'm teaching Darcy and Allie every chance I get."

"So," Ian said, "all those dancing lessons are finally going to pay off."

"Sort of," Stephanie said. "I took jazz, tap, and ballet, but we're doing hip hop for the talent show."

Ian laughed. "Sounds good."

"Hey," said Stephanie, "I heard you won your basketball game against Berkeley Junior High."

"Yup," Ian replied, his eyes lighting up.

"Did you score any points?" she asked him.

"A couple," he answered, looking down at his paper plate.

Stephanie noticed that Ian looked uncomfortable, almost hiding behind the dark hair that fell over his forehead. *Probably he doesn't want to brag about how many points he scored*, she thought. He was one of the top players on the team.

"Umm, Stephanie?" Ian said, looking up and into her eyes. "I've been, uh, wanting to ask you something."

Stephanie was just about to reply when the back door swung open and everyone came back out from the kitchen, including Comet, the Tanners' golden retriever. Jesse carried the cake, and

Becky, D.J., and Michelle carried paper plates and plastic forks.

Stephanie looked curiously at Ian and said, "What did you—"

"Boy, that looks great!" Ian interrupted. "Let me help you with that, Michelle." He stood up abruptly, took the plates from Michelle, and began passing them out.

For a moment Stephanie wondered what Ian had been about to ask her, but then her thoughts drifted back to the talent show and how she just *had* to beat the Flamingoes. Stephanie had once been desperate to join the Flamingoes—until she'd found out that the club of eighth-grade girls wasn't all it was cracked up to be. Jenni Morris, the club leader, had told Stephanie she could become a member if she performed three harmless dares—dares that didn't turn out to be one bit harmless. That sneaky eighth grader had only one thing on her mind: to take advantage of Stephanie's friendship and trick her into stealing her father's phone credit card for her and her Flamingo friends to use.

Then the eighth graders—led by Jenni Morris and the Flamingoes—had made more money than the sixth graders in the fund-raiser for the library, winning a whole day off from school. Jenni had all the teachers at school fooled. They thought she was the sweetest thing in the world. Stephanie had sworn to her friends that she'd get revenge. And now she had the perfect opportunity—she was a better dancer than Jenni any day, and she'd prove it at the talent show.

"I can't wait," Stephanie said out loud. "I just can't wait!"

"There's no reason to wait, Steph," Joey said. "Just chow down on that cake. Everybody else has finished theirs."

Stephanie looked up and saw that everyone at the table was watching her and laughing. She hadn't realized she'd spoken out loud or that she'd been so caught up in her thoughts that she hadn't touched her cake. With a little shrug, she picked up her fork and started in.

The others all began clearing the table and bringing things into the kitchen. Soon only Ian was left, and it seemed to Stephanie that he was watching her intently from his side of the picnic table. She took another bite of cake and looked at him curiously.

"You . . . you want a bite?" she asked.

"Oh—no thanks," Ian said with a half-smile. "Listen, uh, Stephanie, I was wondering . . ."

Stephanie looked up at him, her hand poised with a piece of cake midway to her mouth. She knitted her eyebrows together and waited. Finally she said, "What were you wondering, Ian?"

"Would you go out with me?"

CHAPTER
2

♦ ◂ ◆ ♦

"Out where?" Stephanie asked, puzzled. "We're already outside, Ian. This is a barbecue, remember?"

"Out," repeated Ian, "as in 'out on a date.' With me."

"A date? With you?" Stephanie knew she sounded like a parrot, but she just couldn't think of what to say. She couldn't believe that Ian, a boy she'd known since the days when getting dressed up meant putting on a clean bib, was asking her out.

"Right," Ian continued. "As in, 'Do you want to go out with me after the basketball game Thursday night?' We could go for ice cream or something."

Stephanie put down her forkful of cake. She couldn't believe her ears. No one had ever asked her out on a real date before. Sure, she'd gone to the movies with a whole bunch of kids, including guys, but that was a group thing. Not a *real* date, like her older sister, D.J., went on with her boyfriend, Steve. To Stephanie, a first date was a big deal, something to remember all her life. Was she up to a *real* date? And if so, should it be with *Ian*?

"Well?" Ian asked.

Stephanie felt her face getting hot. She was glad it was almost dark—she knew she was turning red. "Um ... I ..."

"Hey, Steph!" A voice floated across the twilight.

Stephanie turned and saw her two best friends, Allie Taylor and Darcy Powell, coming across the backyard toward her.

"What are you guys doing out here all alone?" Darcy asked.

"It's almost dark and everybody is inside," Allie added.

Stephanie wished her friends wouldn't point

out the obvious—it was making her even more uncomfortable.

Ian swung his leg over the picnic bench and said, "I guess I should get going." Then he stood, as if waiting for an answer from Stephanie.

Stephanie got to her feet too. "I'll . . . uh, talk to you soon, Ian. Okay? I need, you know, a little time to think."

"Okay." Ian shrugged. "See you Monday."

"Okay." Stephanie let out a big breath as Ian walked away.

"What was *that* all about?" Darcy asked. "What do you need a little time to think about?"

Stephanie was saved from answering as Ian's parents called out their good-byes to her through the back door.

After she waved good-bye to the Ezrattys, Stephanie turned to Darcy and Allie. "So, let's go start practicing."

"But what did Ian ask you?" Darcy said, not letting the matter go as Stephanie had hoped she would.

"Tell," Allie begged.

"Oh, it was just something about his basketball game," said Stephanie. "Now listen," she added, opening the back door for her friends, "the talent show is only two weeks away, and we've got some serious work to do."

Once in the living room, Stephanie popped a cassette into her portable tape player. "Ready?"

"Stephanie Tanner, you're keeping a secret from us," Darcy said. "What did he *really* say?"

"You can tell us," Allie crooned. "We can keep a secret."

Allie and Darcy settled down comfortably on the sofa, more ready for a nice long chat than a dance practice. Darcy propped her feet up on the coffee table.

"Come on, guys!" Stephanie pushed her friend's feet off the table. "It's time to boogie!"

"As soon as you tell us," Darcy and Allie said together.

Stephanie hesitated, then gave in—it was two against one. "Okay, okay. You win," she said. "See, Ian kind of asked me out on . . . sort of a date."

"A date?" D.J. said, coming into the living room. "Cool!"

Stephanie shot her sister a look. "I didn't know *you* were listening in!"

"I didn't mean to," D.J. said, "but it *is* cool . . . isn't it?"

"I guess." Stephanie plopped down on the couch beside Allie. "He wants me to go out for ice cream with him after his basketball game on Thursday night."

Stephanie then heard a little voice cry, "Ice cream?"

There, in the corner of the living room, Stephanie now noticed seven-year-old Michelle for the first time.

"Wow, ice cream," Michelle repeated. "He must *really* like you. Can I come?"

"No!" Stephanie shouted, and Michelle turned and ran from the room. "Hey, Michelle! Wait! I didn't mean to yell . . ."

"*And?*" Allie asked impatiently.

"And what?" Stephanie said.

"And what did you *say*?" Darcy shrieked.

"You heard me," Stephanie said. "That I'd have to think about it. So what's the big deal, anyway?"

"Oh, get a load of Miss Cool," Darcy remarked.

"Really," Allie said. "You'd never know she'd just been asked out by a seventh-grade hunk."

17

"Hunk?" Stephanie echoed.

"My little girl!" Danny gushed as he charged into the living room. "Going on her first date! Michelle just told me. I think it's great that you and Ian are going out for ice cream."

"Hold it!" Stephanie sprang up from the couch. "First of all, Ian only asked me—I haven't said yes. And second, I didn't know my conversation with Allie and Darcy was a family activity. Can't a person have some privacy around here?"

"That Ian," Danny said, as if he hadn't heard his daughter. "What a nice boy. You know, he even offered to help with the dishes before he left tonight." Danny turned to Allie and Darcy. "I've known his father for years," he went on. "Did I ever tell you about the time Mike Ezratty, Joey, and I went to the Grand Canyon during spring break and—"

"You fell and sprained your leg, and Joey and Steve had to carry you for nearly three miles," D.J. finished for him.

"A zillion times!" Stephanie added. "You've also told us a zillion times what a 'nice boy' Ian is. But I don't know if I'm going to go out with him. I told him I'd think about it. Now, can we please talk about something else?" She looked at Darcy and Allie. "Like the talent show, maybe?"

"Oh, sure, sweetie," Danny said, heading for the kitchen. "I'll leave you girls alone. Hey, I know ... I'll go ring up Mike and see if the Ezrattys want to come over and watch the game on Friday. We can have pizza."

"Whatever," Stephanie said, as her father headed for the kitchen. Then, turning to her friends, she said, "C'mon, guys, our dance starts with a head roll." Stephanie hit the button on her boom box and took her position. The music blared, and she started dancing. But as she spun around, she saw Darcy and Allie just standing in front of the sofa, staring at her.

Stephanie put her face in her hands and shook her head. Then she marched over to the boom box and hit the off switch. "What? Why are you two looking at me like that?" she demanded.

Darcy walked over to Stephanie and put her hand on her friend's forehead. "Nope," she said, looking at Allie. "No fever."

"What in the world are you talking about?" Stephanie asked.

19

"We just wanted to make sure you were okay," Allie said.

"Yeah," Darcy added. "We figured you must be coming down with something when you tell one of the cutest guys in school you'll have to *think* about going out with him! Don't you like Ian, Steph?"

"Of course I like him." Stephanie frowned. "He's always been a good friend. I don't know if I can think of him as a date, though." She turned to her older sister. "D.J., what would *you* do?"

D.J. considered her sister's predicament. "It would be a real date, Steph. I thought you were dying to go on a real date with a cute, older boy. Don't you think he's cute?"

"I've never really thought about Ian that way, but yeah, I guess he's cute," Stephanie replied.

"Ian's gorgeous!" Darcy butted in. "Do you know how many sixth graders would love to go out with him?"

"Not to mention seventh graders," Allie added. "Ian's a really nice . . . whoops, sorry . . . a really *sweet* guy, too. You don't know how lucky you are."

Maybe her friends were right, Stephanie thought. Maybe most girls in her class would die to get a chance to date Ian Ezratty.

"So, are you going to go or not?" Darcy asked.

Stephanie had to admit she was feeling flattered. She'd spent lots of time with Ian before and had loads of fun. She hadn't realized he was interested in her as . . . as more than a friend . . . as a date. She found herself wondering what had changed her from a friend to a date in his eyes. Was it something she said? Something she wore? Was it because she was getting older? If they went out on a date, would Ian act different? And how would he expect her to act? Something inside her didn't feel quite right about this.

Allie cut into her thoughts. "So, what are you going to tell him, Steph?"

"What kind of ice cream are you going to have?" added Michelle, who had just come back into the room. "Are you going to have sprinkles?"

"Or you could share a banana split," Darcy added.

Stephanie couldn't stop herself from giggling along with the girls. She found herself wondering what she should wear. *Will D.J. let me borrow her stretch lace bodysuit? Will Dad let me stay out a little later, since it's a real date?*

"Stephanie, it's Darcy . . . Over. Can you read me?" Darcy said, pulling on her friend's sleeve.

Stephanie snapped back to the present as Allie asked her again what she planned to say to Ian.

"I don't know yet," she said finally. "Come on, it's rehearsal time."

CHAPTER
3

◆ ◀ ◗ ◆

On Monday morning Stephanie and Allie watched Darcy come skipping down the hall toward them, her thick black curls bouncing with every step. Darcy hardly ever *walked* anywhere—she almost always skipped or ran. Stephanie thought Darcy had more energy than she and Allie put together.

Stephanie and Allie had met Darcy a year ago when the Powells had moved to San Francisco from Chicago. The threesome had hit it off right from the start, and now they did almost everything together.

"Today's the day we sign up for the talent

show," Darcy said as she came sliding to a stop in front of Stephanie and Allie.

"I can sign up during study hall," Stephanie offered. "Maybe I can find out what the competition is like—I mean aside from the Flamingoes."

"Okay, and you'll let us know at lunch," Allie said. "I gotta get going." She started off to her next class.

"Wait a minute!" Stephanie said. "When's our next practice?"

"Practice?" a snooty voice called out from behind them. "Why bother?"

The sixth-grade girls turned toward the voice. There, standing with two friends by the drinking fountain, was Jenni Morris.

"You three are not seriously thinking of entering the talent show, are you?" Jenni let out her high-and-mighty "I'm-superior-to-you" laugh, and her friends copied her.

Stephanie felt anger building up inside. "You know we are," she answered.

"Well, too bad," Jenni said with a cool, smug smile. "A few of us Flamingoes already have a totally hot dance number for the show. We even have our costumes made, and they're awesome!

Besides, we've been working on our routine for weeks now . . . there's no way we can lose!"

They have costumes already? Stephanie thought in dismay. "Well, for your information," she replied, her voice shaking slightly, "we've been working on our routine, too. For *months*." At least Stephanie felt as if it had been months. "Isn't that right, guys?" she asked, nudging Darcy.

"Right!" Darcy chimed in. "It's really an awesome routine."

Jenni's smug smile faded, and she motioned to her friends that it was time to go. "Don't bother entering anyway," she said, flipping her long brown hair over her shoulder. "I happen to know for a fact that you three don't have a chance of winning!"

"She makes me *so* mad!" Stephanie exclaimed as she watched the eighth grader saunter down the hall.

"I know exactly what you mean," Darcy said.

"But I know we can beat them," Stephanie said firmly. "We'll practice today after school for an extra hour. Okay, guys?"

25

"Okay," Darcy said, walking down the hall with Allie.

"See you at lunch, Steph," Allie called over her shoulder.

As she stood in front of the secretary's desk in the principal's office, Stephanie reached down and massaged her aching calf. After last night's practice for the talent show, she had to admit her muscles were pretty sore.

"May I help you, young lady?"

Stephanie straightened up and smiled at the school secretary. "Yes, Ms. Zotos. I'd like to sign up for the talent show, please."

"Okay." Ms. Zotos pointed a finger behind her to a sign-up sheet that was attached to a clipboard on the wall. "Just fill in your name and the type and title of your act."

Stephanie gazed at the dozens of acts already signed up. There were singers, dancers, musicians, a magic act, and even a stand-up comic. Then she spotted Jenni Morris's name opposite the "Flamingo Dancers." Stephanie made a face, but she was pretty confident that the routine she, Allie, and Darcy had worked on all weekend was coming along great. Still, the Flamingoes already had costumes . . .

Stephanie simply wrote "dance" under type of act and signed her name. Since they hadn't come up with a name for themselves yet, she left that part blank. She started to ask Ms. Zotos if it was okay to fill that part in later, but the secretary was nowhere in sight. The computer on her desk *was* in sight, though, and something on the screen caught Stephanie's eye.

Student Judges for the Talent Show
Grade 6: Debra Mostow
Grade 7: Ian Ezratty
Grade 8: Darah Judson

"Can I help you with something else?" Ms. Zotos said, suddenly beside Stephanie.

Embarrassed that she'd been caught snooping, Stephanie mumbled, "N-no, thank you. I, um, I guess I'll be going to lunch. Thank you."

As she walked to the cafeteria Stephanie thought, *So, Ian is one of the judges. Why didn't he tell me that at the barbecue?* She'd been trying to avoid thinking about Ian. Sure, she was flattered that he was interested in her, but she still didn't know if she wanted to go out on a date with him. But as Darcy, Allie, and D.J. had pointed out, who could resist a real date with an older guy? People would see her out with a seventh grader at the ice-cream place and word would get out at school that they were dating. And when she thought about it, she had to admit that Ian really *was* cute. There was a bounce in Stephanie's walk as she hurried to the cafeteria.

Allie and Darcy were already at their favorite lunch table, waiting for her. They hadn't begun eating yet—they were trying their hardest to wait till Stephanie got there before they started their lunch.

"Finally!" Darcy wailed when Stephanie threw her bag on the table. "I'm starved!" Within seconds, Darcy had torn open her lunch bag and stuffed one of her two tuna-and-cheese sandwiches into her mouth. Allie and Stephanie watched her in amazement.

"How do you stay so skinny?" Stephanie asked, shaking her head and laughing. "Darcy, you have an appetite like a horse!"

"It's my metabolism," Darcy mumbled.

Allie giggled and opened her lunch bag. She stopped to rub her shoulder. "Is anyone else as sore as I am?" she asked.

Stephanie groaned and reached down to her calf. "Yeah, I could barely walk to the bus stop this morning!"

"You're telling me!" Darcy said in between bites. "I couldn't even lift my book bag."

"Well, it'll get better," Stephanie assured them.

"So what happened, Steph?" Allie asked. "Did you sign us up?"

"Yep," Stephanie replied. "Only I had to leave a blank where it asked for our group name. We have to come up with one right away, though, so start thinking of possibilities. And, Darcy, you still want to be in charge of costumes?"

"Definitely," Darcy said. "I'm working on it."

"Okay," Stephanie said. "Here's the big news. While I was at the office, I accidentally snuck a peek at the list of student judges for the talent show."

Allie and Darcy stopped eating. "And?" Darcy asked.

"The eighth-grade judge is Darah Judson," Stephanie said.

Allie groaned. "Oh, no! Not a Flamingo!"

Stephanie'd been so flustered when she saw Ian's name on the list that she'd forgotten about Darah's Flamingo connection.

"Well, that's one vote we can forget about," Darcy said. "She's one of Jenni's closest friends."

Allie slumped in her chair. "There's no way Darah Judson would ever vote for us," she said glumly. "Even if we're excellent and Jenni's group totally messes up. This is not good, Stephanie. Not good at all."

"What about the sixth-grade judge?" Darcy asked.

"It's Debra Mostow," Stephanie told them. "I don't know her, but maybe she'll vote for us since she's a sixth grader."

"I know her," Darcy said. "She's that new girl from Florida. I talked to her in that assembly we had in the gym a couple of weeks ago. She's really nice. She's got strawberry blond hair with bangs, and she's about my height—no, maybe shorter, and—"

"You mean her?" Allie asked, pointing behind them.

Stephanie and Darcy turned in their seats and followed Allie's finger. Sure enough, there was Debra Mostow, sitting at the Flamingoes' select table, laughing it up with Jenni Morris!

All three girls gasped. Darcy moaned, "We're doomed!"

"So who's the seventh-grade judge, Steph?" Allie asked.

Stephanie sighed. She knew she'd have to say it sooner or later, so she decided to get it over with. "Ian Ezratty," she said in a small voice.

"Oh," Darcy said with a laugh. "I guess we know who lover boy is going to vote for."

"Would you give me a break?" Stephanie said, turning red.

"Oooh, blushing! Looks like true love to me!" Allie joked.

"Maybe I put on a little too much makeup this morning," Stephanie mumbled.

"We *know* you never wear makeup, Steph," Darcy said. "You can't fool us." Darcy kicked Allie under the table, and they both started cracking up.

"Will you two knock it off?" Stephanie said. "I mean, please! He only asked me out for ice cream."

Allie looked down at her half-eaten sandwich and said, "Well, one vote is better than none."

"But one out of three might as well be none," Darcy said.

"You're right," Stephanie added with a sigh. "How are we ever going to beat the Flamingoes?"

CHAPTER
4

"Pass me those cookies, Allie," Darcy said, lying on Stephanie's bed with her feet propped up on the wall.

"Here, catch," Allie said, tossing her the box of chocolate-chip cookies.

"When I'm worried, I can polish off a whole box of these things," Darcy said.

"Save some for me," Allie said as she flopped onto the other side of the bed.

"Will you guys keep it down?" Stephanie demanded. "If my father catches us eating up here, he'll ground me for life!"

"That would be great," Darcy said. "Then

we wouldn't have to compete in the talent show."

"What are we going to do now?" Allie asked. "We might as well just drop out of the competition."

"Yeah, two out of three judges against us doesn't look very promising," Stephanie agreed, falling onto Michelle's bed with a thud. "It's so unfair. I mean, we've put so much work into this already. My arms are so achy, I can barely brush my teeth!"

Just then there was a knock at the door. "Come in," Stephanie said.

D.J. bounced in, eager to show the girls her new baggy denim cutoffs. But when she saw Stephanie and her friends drooped all over the beds, she stopped in her tracks.

"What's wrong?" D.J. asked. "The three of you look like poor little puppy dogs. Or like your favorite TV show was canceled."

"Worse," Allie said.

"It's the talent show," Darcy explained. "We're thinking of dropping out."

D.J. was shocked. "Why? You worked all weekend on that En Vogue thing. If I hear the song one more time, I think I might lose it completely. Anyway, I thought you guys were great."

"We found out who the three judges for the show are," Stephanie explained. "And two of them are definitely not voting for us."

When Stephanie told her sister who the judges were, D.J. said, "That's your reason for quitting? Are you crazy? You're not going to compete because you think two judges might not vote for you?"

Stephanie shrugged and toyed with a lock of her hair.

"Steph, that's not like you. You can't enter a competition based on what you think the judges might do," said D.J. "If you go out onstage and put on a really excellent show and totally flip everyone out, the judges will *have* to vote for you. Anyway, you have to at least try."

Stephanie lifted herself off the bed. "She's right, you know," she said to Allie and Darcy. "We can't give up without trying first. We can put together a much better show than Jenni. I'm sure we can. Even if we are a little bit sore."

Darcy laughed. "A little bit? I feel like I just

rolled down Mount Everest." Then she said, "But I'm into it if you are."

"Count me in too," Allie said. "But you'll have to help me off this bed first."

Grabbing Allie's hands, Stephanie pulled her friend up, but Stephanie lost her balance and both girls tumbled to the floor.

"You guys are pathetic!" D.J. laughed. "I'll help you if you like."

"Really, D.J.?" Stephanie brightened slightly. "C'mon," she said to Allie and Darcy. "We've already wasted half the afternoon sulking! We have a lot of catching up to do."

The four girls bounded down the stairs two at a time, then D.J. helped Stephanie shove the coffee table out of the way to set up their rehearsal space. Stephanie popped the En Vogue tape into the boom box and the girls took their positions in the middle of the living room: Stephanie front and center, Allie to her right, and Darcy to her left.

"Let's see what you've got so far," D.J. said, settling into the nearest chair to watch.

"Hi, everybody! What's going on?"

The girls looked up to see Michelle standing

in the doorway. She was wearing her pink tutu and a sparkling tiara.

"Hi, Michelle," Allie said. "You look so cute!"

Michelle spun around to show off her costume. "I had ballet today," she told them. "Wanna see what I learned?"

"Not now, Michelle," Stephanie said. "We have work to do."

"What are you doing?" Michelle asked.

"We have to practice real hard for our talent show," Stephanie explained.

Michelle's eyes lit up. "A talent show? Oh, can I be in it too? Please, Stephanie? Please, please, please?"

"Sorry, Michelle," Stephanie said. "It's for junior high only."

"But I have a really good act!" Michelle persisted. "I learned it in class today. It's for our recital. Wanna see it?" She got into position as if she were about to dance.

"Later, Michelle," Stephanie insisted.

"But—" Michelle began.

"Michelle!" Stephanie snapped. "Enough's enough!"

"Come over here, Michelle," D.J. said, shooting a look at Stephanie. "You can squeeze in by me on this chair and watch."

"Sorry, Michelle," Stephanie apologized. "I didn't mean to be cranky. It's just that we're so far behind schedule." She sighed. "Okay, are we ready?" Allie and Darcy nodded, and Stephanie flipped on the tape player.

The music began again, and for almost thirty seconds D.J. and Michelle watched as the girls stood in the middle of the living room with their heads down, not moving.

"Why aren't they dancing?" Michelle whispered loudly to D.J.

"I don't know," D.J. whispered back.

"This isn't a very good routine," Michelle said.

Stephanie walked over to the boom box and punched the button off again. "We're not dancing," she said between clenched teeth, "because I haven't worked out the introduction yet."

"How come?" Michelle asked.

"Because," Stephanie answered as calmly as she could, "I . . . I haven't thought of anything good enough yet."

Michelle jumped off the chair. "Stephanie, I know a great introduction! I'm doing it for our ballet recital next week. Here, I'll show it to you, then you can use it too!"

"Michelle, we don't want to use your introduction! Please, sit down with D.J. and don't get in the way." Stephanie drew a deep breath, then said in a sweet tone, "Now just pretend we have an intro, okay?" For the third time, she turned on the tape. But when the song got to the same place where they'd been interrupted before, Danny Tanner burst into the living room holding out the portable phone.

"Steph, it's Ian," he said, grinning.

"Ian?" Allie asked. She and Darcy exchanged knowing glances, and Darcy said, "Wonder what lover boy wants."

"Oh, grow up!" Stephanie told her, shooting a cross look at her friends. *This is so embarrassing!* she thought. "Dad, can't you tell him I'm busy?"

"Stephanie!" Allie yelped. "At least see what he wants!"

Stephanie grabbed the phone, then moved to the other side of the living room for a little privacy. She'd talked to Ian on the phone dozens of times before and it had been no big deal. But with everyone standing right in the room, and with the big "date" hanging in the air, this time she felt flustered.

"Hi, Ian," she whispered. "What? Oh, yeah. I, um . . . uh . . ." She felt her face getting redder by the second and tried to lower her voice even more. "Listen," she said. "I can't really talk right now. Darcy and Allie are here and we're rehearsing. Okay, bye."

Stephanie switched off the phone and turned around.

Everybody in the room was staring at her.

"Well? What did he say?" her father finally asked.

"He just said . . . he'd talk to me in school tomorrow."

"Well, he is a very nice boy," Danny said. "Did I tell you how he offered to do the dish—"

"Yes, Dad, you did," Stephanie said, forcing a smile. As her father left the room Stephanie said, "Let's get go—"

"Hold everything!" Darcy said. "I just got an idea."

"You have a name for our act?" Stephanie said hopefully.

"No, but I have an idea how we can win this thing. Steph, you can convince Ian to have a talk with Debra, the sixth-grade judge. Ian can tell Debra how hard we've been practicing and how good we are."

"Yeah, Steph. Tell Ian how bad the Flamingoes really are," Allie added. "Tell him that they've been using Debra for her vote, and then he can tell Debra what the Flamingoes are all about."

"All you have to do is have a little talk with him, Steph," said Darcy, "when you go out for ice cream."

"It's our only hope, Stephanie," Allie added. "Debra might listen to reason—especially if it's coming from a hunk like Ian."

Stephanie bit her lip and looked at her friends. She didn't want to let them down. But why was she dreading talking to Ian?

"It's the only way, Steph," said Darcy. "You've got to talk to Ian."

CHAPTER
5

"Hey, Steph!" Darcy greeted her friend as she stood before her locker in the school hallway. "So, have you decided yet?"

Stephanie let her heavy book bag drop into her locker. It landed with a thud. She couldn't wait for her history exam to be over with. Lugging that heavy history book was really a pain, especially with her aching muscles. "You mean about a name for our act?"

"You know very well what I mean," Darcy coaxed. "Ian's a dream date *and* the only chance we have. You've got to tell him to talk to Debra."

Steph sighed and made a face at her friend.

Allie came up behind Stephanie and poked her in the ribs. "So, what's the story? To ice cream or not to ice cream? That is the question!"

Stephanie glared at Allie.

"I don't get it, Steph," Allie said. "You always talk about how much fun you and Ian have with your families and all. What's the big deal, anyway? It's only ice cream after a basketball game."

Stephanie knew Allie was right. But something was holding her back from talking to Ian. She wasn't sure what. She only knew that now she felt confused when anyone even mentioned his name. There was only one thing to do: change the subject. "Now listen," she said with authority. "Did anybody come up with a good name?"

"I did!" Darcy said. "How about the Red Hot Dancers?"

Stephanie frowned and said, "I don't know . . . it sounds too much like the Red Hot Chili Peppers. What about the Beat Babes?"

"The Beat Babes?" Darcy asked, making a disapproving face. "That's dumb. What about the Funky Foxes?"

"Now that's *really* dumb," Stephanie retorted.

"Well, your idea wasn't any better, Stephanie," Darcy said.

Stephanie sniffed. "I happen to like the Beat Babes." She turned to Allie. "Did you come up with anything?"

"What about the Hip Hop Girls?" Allie offered shyly.

Darcy smiled. "Hey, I like that!"

"Yeah, me too!" Stephanie said. "Finally we can agree on *something*. I guess that's it, then. The Hip Hop Girls. Let's see how it sounds." She cleared her throat and said loudly, "Ladies and gentlemen, we are happy to introduce the coolest dance act in all of San Francisco! In all—"

Suddenly Darcy grabbed Stephanie's sleeve and whispered, "Look who's coming toward us!"

As the three looked down the hall they saw Jenni Morris, like a bad dream, heading in their direction.

"Isn't that Debra Mostow with her?" Stephanie asked. "What . . . are they best friends now?"

"Let's make a run for it!" Darcy said. But it was too late. Jenni was making a beeline for the group.

"Still considering entering the talent show?" Jenni called out.

"That's right," Stephanie said, trying to sound confident. "We've put together an excellent routine."

"Well, you'll still need a miracle to win," Jenni retorted. "The Flamingo Dancers are the best! By the way," she added as if she'd just remembered, "have you met Debra Mostow? She's the newest member of the Flamingoes!"

Debra smiled at them, but all Stephanie, Allie, and Darcy could do was stare back at her with gaping mouths.

"C'mon, Debra," Jenni said, "we have some important Flamingo business to take care of." She then led a slightly confused-looking Debra away by the arm.

"Bye!" Debra called over her shoulder. "Nice meeting you!"

"Poor Debra . . ." Allie said, her voice trailing off.

"How typical of Jenni to make her a Flamingo," Darcy added. "Do you think Debra had to pass the initiation?" she asked Stephanie.

"Nah," Stephanie said. "I'll bet Jenni made her

a Flamingo just to get another vote for the Flamingo Dancers. I wouldn't put it past Jenni to do something that nasty. Watch . . . she'll probably drop Debra pronto right after the show!"

"Well, if that's true, I feel bad for Debra," Allie said. "She seems like such a nice person."

"All the more reason you should ask Ian to have a little chat with Debra, Steph," Darcy said. "One judge to another."

Suddenly Allie's eyes widened and a strange smile crossed her face. "Don't look now, Steph, but guess who's on his way over here at this very minute!"

"Who?" Stephanie asked.

"Ian!"

Stephanie folded her arms across her chest and raised an eyebrow. "Yeah, right, Alison. Very funny."

"No, really! I swear!"

"That's not funny, Al—" But before Stephanie could say another word, she heard Ian's familiar voice behind her.

"Hey, Stephanie," he said. "What's up?"

Stephanie spun around. "Oh . . . Ian. Hi!" She realized her voice was cracking. *Why am I so ner-*

vous all of a sudden? she wondered. "So, how are you?"

He smiled. "I'm okay. Listen, can I talk to you for a sec?"

"We're leaving," Darcy said, grabbing Allie by the arm.

"Oh, don't leave," Ian said. "I just wanted to check with Stephanie on what's happening after the game Thursday night."

Darcy and Allie froze where they were.

Boy, Stephanie thought, *talk about putting somebody on the spot!* She looked over at Allie and Darcy, who were waiting to hear what she was going to say. The whole situation—Ian acting different from his old, comfortable self, Allie and Darcy acting as if this were the biggest moment in her life—made her mad. Well, she'd had enough!

"Actually, Ian," Stephanie said, "Thursday isn't good for me. I have to baby-sit for Nicky and Alex."

No sooner were the words out of her mouth than Stephanie was sorry. She stared at the floor. She'd just *lied* to Ian! How could she have done that? She felt Darcy and Allie's stares, but couldn't bring herself to look at them. They knew she didn't have to baby-sit.

"Oh, well, okay," Ian said. "No problem. I mean, if you're busy, you're busy. Maybe another time."

Stephanie finally looked up into his eyes. She tried to smile. "Yeah, maybe another time," she offered.

"Okay," Ian said. "Well, see you around."

As soon as he turned the corner and was out of sight, Stephanie put up her hand to stop her friends from saying a word. "Just don't say it," she warned. "I don't know why I told Ian I had to baby-sit, but I did, and from this point on we are not discussing Ian Ezratty anymore. Don't even bother bringing him up, because I won't talk about him. Understood?"

Allie and Darcy looked wide-eyed at Stephanie.

"But, Steph—" Darcy began.

"We are not talking about it anymore," Stephanie said. "I want your word. Promise?"

"Promise," Allie said reluctantly.

"Promise," Darcy echoed with a sigh.

CHAPTER
6

◆ ▼ ◂ ◆

"I'm sorry," D.J. said for the tenth time. "I didn't know Steve was going to get these concert tickets for tonight. If I had known, I never would have promised to help you guys rehearse today. But I am not going to miss a Janet Jackson concert just to watch you and your friends dance around the living room!" Outside, D.J.'s boyfriend, Steve, honked the car horn again, this time a little longer.

"I gotta go," D.J. said. "Steve's waiting."

"You want me to put the music on?" Michelle asked. She'd been sitting patiently beside the boom box, her finger on the on/off button, waiting for her cue. She'd begged so pitifully for Stephanie to let her in on the rehearsal that afternoon that Stephanie had finally agreed. She'd even given Michelle a big responsibility: turning the music on and off, mainly to keep her quiet and out of the way.

"Not yet, Michelle," Stephanie answered. "Come on, Darcy! Get into position, already!"

"Stephanie," Darcy said angrily, "why are you so *snippy* today? You're not still mad at me for having to miss our rehearsal tomorrow, are you?"

Stephanie flopped down on the couch. "I'm not *mad* at you," she said. "It's just that we're not making much progress. How are we supposed to beat Jenni Morris if we don't rehearse?"

"Well, I can't miss my lacrosse practice," Darcy said.

Stephanie waved her hand. "Just forget it, okay? Can we please get started?" She checked that Allie was in position, then she turned to cue Michelle.

"Now?" Michelle asked.

"Yes, now."

Michelle turned on the music and waited. But

50

once again, for the first thirty seconds the girls just stood there.

"You still don't have an introduction?" Michelle called out over the music.

Stephanie glared at her. "I'm working on it!" Then she counted out loud: "One, two, three, *and*!" All at once, the girls began to dance.

"Right knee to the floor!" Stephanie called. "Left knee to the floor—spin to the right—arms up high—back up on your feet—and kick . . ."

Suddenly there was a thud and a cry of pain. Darcy was on the floor, clutching her shin.

"Who put that coffee table there?" Darcy winced.

"You and I did—five minutes ago," Stephanie said. "How did you bump into it? You should've been going the *other* way after the kick."

Allie ran to Darcy's side. "Are you okay, Darce?"

Darcy inspected her shin, which was turning red. "It hurts," she said.

"Here, let me help you try to stand up," Allie offered.

With Allie's arm around her, Darcy hobbled

around the room, wincing. "It hurts," she repeated, "but I think I can walk on it."

"Can you *dance* on it?" Stephanie asked impatiently.

Allie glared at her. "Stephanie, why don't you get her some ice or something?"

"Okay," Stephanie said. "I'm sorry."

Stephanie returned from the kitchen with a bag of ice, then helped Darcy over to the sofa. "Sit for a while and put your leg up on this pillow." Stephanie placed the ice on Darcy's shin.

"Thanks, Steph," Darcy said. "Hey, I've got an idea. You guys keep dancing, and I'll watch from here and give you some pointers."

"But you don't know the choreography," Stephanie objected.

"I can tell what works," Darcy said. "And what stinks."

"Oh, oh, oh! Can I take Darcy's place?" Michelle asked. "Please, Steph!"

Stephanie sighed. "I guess. But just for today," she warned.

"Hooray!" Michelle looked positively thrilled.

"So what do you say, Stephanie?" Darcy asked

again. "I'll be the dance critic for today, seeing as D.J. couldn't make it."

"I don't know . . ." Stephanie said, her voice trailing off.

"Just because you're the best dancer," Darcy said angrily, "doesn't mean you get to do everything! I have some ideas too, you know! Who put you in charge anyway?"

"Look, we agreed that you'd do costumes and I'd do choreography," Stephanie said. "Anyway," she added, "I *do* have the most dance experience."

"Well, lah-dee-dah!" Darcy said.

"Guys! C'mon," Allie pleaded. "Stop fighting."

"You're no Paula Abdul, Stephanie!" Darcy said.

"I never said I was!" Stephanie shot back. "And if you can't even bother to make it to rehearsals, then why should *you* be the one to give *us* pointers?"

"I *have* to go to lacrosse practice!" Darcy said.

"This is more important than dumb lacrosse practice!" Stephanie insisted. "You promised to be at every rehearsal. If Jenni and the Flamingo

Dancers win the competition, it'll be all your fault!"

"*My* fault?" Darcy cried. "Because I missed one stupid rehearsal? Listen, if the Flamingoes win, it'll be because your choreography was the pits!"

"Darcy!" Allie gasped in horror.

"Well, I'm sorry, but she started it!" Darcy exclaimed. "Why does she get to choreograph the whole thing anyway?"

"You should let Darcy make up some steps, Stephanie," Michelle said.

"Mind your own business, Michelle!" Stephanie yelled, and then she put her head in her hands. *This day has been just peachy,* she thought. She knew she was being moody, but who wouldn't be? She was sure she'd failed her history exam, she'd blown the whole thing with Ian, and neither Allie nor Darcy seemed to be taking the talent competition seriously at all. Didn't they realize how important it was to beat the Flamingoes? Stephanie's dancing reputation was at stake—not to mention the good name of the sixth grade—plus she wanted to give snotty Jenni Morris a good dose of her own medicine!

"I don't know what's gotten into you," Allie said, "but you're both acting like big babies! Who cares if we win or lose—I thought we were in this to have *fun*!"

Stephanie stared at her friend as the words sank in. "You're right, Allie," she said quietly. "I'm sorry, Darcy. I'm just bummed out. Of course you can give us pointers, and then D.J. can help us out when we're all here together. Meanwhile, we should—"

"Uh, Stephanie?" Allie said meekly.

"What is it, Allie?"

"I can't rehearse on Friday after school. That's when I have my piano lesson."

"Oh, boy," Michelle said eagerly. "Can I take Allie's place on Friday?"

"And I already have plans on Friday after school," Darcy added. "I can only practice for like an hour or so."

Stephanie was dumbfounded. "Oh, that's great! Just great!" she wailed. "Can't either of you cancel?"

"I made these plans with my sister weeks ago!" Darcy protested.

"What about you, Allie?" Stephanie asked. "Can you cancel your lesson?"

"No way!" Allie said. "You know my mother would kill me."

"Just forget it!" Stephanie yelled. "Maybe we should spend the little time we have together making a congratulations card to give Jenni Morris when her Flamingoes win the talent show!"

That said, Stephanie stormed up the stairs to her bedroom. She slammed the door and threw herself on her bed. From downstairs she heard Darcy say to Allie, "What's wrong with *her*?" and then the front door shut as Darcy and Allie let themselves out.

After a few minutes Stephanie heard a knock on her door and her younger sister's voice. "Stephanie? Can I come in?"

"It's your room too, Michelle," Stephanie said flatly.

Slowly Michelle cracked open the door. "What are you doing?" she asked her older sister.

"Lying on my bed and staring at the ceiling,"

Stephanie answered sarcastically. "What does it look like I'm doing?"

"It looks like you're lying on your bed and staring at the ceiling," Michelle said. "Are you still angry?"

Stephanie sat up slowly and propped her pillow against the wall. Leaning back, she sighed and said, "Oh, I don't know, Michelle. I guess I *am* angry . . . about a lot of things."

"Do you want me to cheer you up?"

"Not now. Maybe later."

"Okay, tell me when you're ready and I'll show you my solo for my dance recital. Miss Black made it up, and it's the best part of the whole show!"

"I'm sure it is," Stephanie said distractedly, her head whirling with her problems. *It's times like this that I wish I had my own room,* Stephanie thought. She had about a zillion things on her mind. How was she going to explain her history grade to her father? How was she going to face Ian when his family came over for pizza Friday night? What if the truth came out about sitting for the twins? And how would she ever make up with Darcy and Allie after being so horrible and rude?

Stephanie groaned and rolled over, burying her face into her pillow. Deep in her heart, she knew she could deal with that list of problems, but the one thing she didn't think she could stand was watching stuck-up Jenni Morris and the Flamingo Dancers win the talent show. The thought of it made her feel sick! Losing the talent show to Jenni would just be the ultimate worst.

Stephanie sat up. "That settles it," she said.

"Settles what?" Michelle asked.

"I've got to pull myself together, Michelle," Stephanie said, "and do everything in my power to make sure the Hip Hop Girls beat the Flamingo Dancers!"

CHAPTER
7

◆ ◂ ◂ ◆

"What do you think, D.J.?" Stephanie asked as she twirled into her big sister's room to model her talent-show costume: a black leotard, black biker shorts, and black sneakers.

From where she sat on her bed, D.J. tilted her head, inspecting the outfit. "It's . . . very . . . *black*," she said at last. "Is that what Darcy came up with?"

"Actually," Stephanie said, "this is more *my* idea. Darcy's still mad about what happened at Tuesday's rehearsal, and we haven't had a chance to talk about costumes. We didn't rehearse yesterday because of lacrosse practice."

D.J. nodded. "From what Michelle told me, you were a little *cranky* on Tuesday. Is Darcy not speaking to you?"

"We're still speaking," Stephanie said, "but I just about had to get on my knees and beg her to come to rehearsal today."

"I'd help out, but I have to study for this English test," D.J. said.

"Oh, thanks, D.J.," Stephanie said, looking at her wristwatch in disgust. "I can't believe they're eight minutes late."

"You can't blame Darcy for being upset," D.J. said. "I mean, all she wants is to feel she's contributing to the act."

"Yeah, I guess," Stephanie said.

"And I thought she was responsible for designing the costumes," D.J. added. "Won't she be mad when she sees you've put together a costume already?"

"But this is the look we should have," Stephanie protested.

Just then the front doorbell rang, and seconds later Danny called up the stairs, "Steph! Allie and Darcy are here."

Stephanie checked her watch again. *"Nine* minutes late."* With that, she headed downstairs.

"Boy, Steph," D.J. called after her, "I hope I don't ever have to work for you!"

Stephanie took a deep breath as she rushed down the stairs, reminding herself not to lose it today. What they had to accomplish was just too important for petty quarreling. "Hey, guys," she said, smiling. "Ready to practice?"

"No more tantrums?" Darcy asked, eyeing her suspiciously.

"Darcy, I apologized a trillion times for that already. I'm sorry for the way I acted." She put her hand on Darcy's shoulder. "Today you will see a totally new and upbeat Stephanie Tanner! A totally agreeable, cheerful, jolly—"

"Stephanie . . ." Allie interrupted. *"What* are you wearing?"

Stephanie spun around with her arms stretched out at her sides. "Could it be our costume for the talent show?"

"Hey!" Darcy cried. "I thought *I* was designing our costumes!"

"You hadn't said anything about it, so I fig-

61

ured you didn't want to do it anymore," Stephanie said.

"Well, you figured wrong!" Darcy said.

"But what's the matter with this?" Stephanie asked. "Don't you like it? I think it's just the look we want."

"What do you mean, *we* want?" Darcy said. Turning to Allie, she added, "See? This is just what I meant. We have to do everything *her* way! She made up the routine and gives herself all the good parts, and now *she's* decided what we're going to wear!"

"Okay!" Stephanie said. "Can you stop talking about me like I'm not here? Forget it—we don't have to wear this if you don't want us to, Darcy. I was just trying to get something done!"

"But that was *my* job!" Darcy went on. "You know I'm much more artistic than you when it comes to designing costumes. You saw the costume I made for my little brother for his play last fall."

"You're not planning on dressing us like trees, are you?" Stephanie asked sarcastically.

Darcy turned to Allie and said, "Do you see what I have to put up with?"

"Okay, Allie, what do you think?" Stephanie asked. "What should we do about the costumes?"

"Oh, no," Allie said. "I am *not* going to be the referee for you two again. Please, do me just one favor," she begged, "and stop bickering!"

"But—" Stephanie began.

Allie put up her hand. "No buts, Stephanie. Darcy's right," she said firmly. "We all agreed that Darcy would be the costume designer. Okay?" She looked pleadingly into Stephanie's eyes.

"Fine," Stephanie said. "But do you think we could *see* some costumes anytime in, say, the next two or three years? The talent show is eight days away!"

"Okay," Darcy said. "I'll admit I've dragged my feet on this a little, but wait'll you see what I'm gonna come up with!"

"Are you going to start dancing soon?" a small voice called out. The older girls turned to see Michelle sitting on the floor, her finger on the boom-box button. The impatient look on her little face made them all start laughing, and the tension in the air evaporated.

"Okay, Michelle," Stephanie said. "Two seconds! But we still don't have an intro, so don't ask!"

Darcy and Allie stripped off their street clothes and adjusted their workout suits. Stephanie kicked off the black sneakers, wiggled out of the black biker shorts, and pulled a bright red extra-long T-shirt over her head. Then they took their positions in the middle of the living room. Stephanie nodded to Michelle. "Ready!"

Michelle hit the button and En Vogue began singing. As the beat of the song sped up, the girls began their dance. Michelle turned the volume way up, and with the beat thrumming through the house, pretty soon Danny and Joey came in from the kitchen to see what was going on. Seconds later D.J. came downstairs to watch, followed by Jesse and Becky, each holding a twin.

"Hey, you kids are pretty good!" Joey remarked.

"Yeah," Becky agreed. "Very professional."

"Careful, Steph!" Danny called. "Watch those dried flowers! I just vacuumed today."

Jesse and Joey looked at each other and

laughed. "You vacuum every day," Joey muttered. Danny just shrugged.

As the music ended the audience applauded, even the twins, who'd been dancing on the sidelines.

"Thank you, thank you," Stephanie said, bowing and throwing kisses. "Dad, did you really like it?" she asked.

"Yes, hon," Danny said. "It was adorable."

"Adorable?" Stephanie made a face. That was not exactly the praise she'd hoped for.

Becky came to Danny's rescue. "What your father means," she said, "is that it was really . . . umm . . . *radical.*"

"I do?" Danny asked, puzzled. Jesse nudged him with an elbow.

"Well, then, it's radically adorable," Danny said.

Everybody groaned.

"I'm sorry! I can't help it," Danny said. "I thought it was adorable. That's a compliment, you know. Isn't it? Adorable is still good, right?"

"Danny, Danny, Danny," Joey said, shaking his head. "You're such a father."

"You're right, Joey," Danny replied. "And

luckily I'm a father who cooks, and a father who could use some help getting dinner on. Any volunteers?''

"Not me, Dad," Stephanie said. "We still have to rehearse."

"Me too, Daddy," Michelle piped up.

"Not me," D.J. said, skipping up the stairs on the way to her bedroom. "I've got to finish this book for English by tomorrow."

"We'll help," Jesse said. "Right, boys?" Nicky and Alex giggled as their father scooped them up in his arms. Becky and Joey followed the three of them into the kitchen.

Stephanie wrinkled her nose. "My father said we were adorable."

"But he liked it," Allie said.

"Adorable means we were cute, like a bunch of little girls," Stephanie said. "And that's just not going to cut it when we're up against older kids."

"What do you suggest, then?" Darcy asked.

Stephanie thought for a moment. "I think," she said finally, "that we have to come off more mature." She looked down at the floor where she'd kicked off her sneakers and biker pants.

"All black is grown-up," she added. "It's the right look for us."

"Here we go again," Allie mumbled.

"All black?" Darcy said. "But that's so boring! I was thinking something colorful, something bright, with sequins and stuff!"

"Yech! Sequins are for Halloween costumes," Stephanie said. "All black is ... sophisticated. We should look like the En Vogue girls do in their videos."

"I think you're wrong," Darcy said. "We need some color."

"No, we don't," Stephanie said, trying to get Darcy to see her point. "Just black will be really cool. Trust me."

Darcy put her hands on her hips. "Stephanie, I am sick to death of your bossy attitude. I don't want to wear all black!"

"Bossy?" Stephanie looked surprised. "Am I bossy, Allie?"

"Sorry," Allie said. "I'm not getting involved anymore."

"The answer is *yes*," Darcy said angrily. "You *are* bossy, and I'm tired of it! I am *not* having fun! I do not want to be in this stupid act one minute longer, and I *quit*!"

In a blur Darcy grabbed her street clothes and her bag and stormed out of the house, leaving Stephanie, Allie, and Michelle staring after her, speechless.

"Wow. I didn't realize she was that mad," Stephanie finally said.

"Do you blame her?" Allie asked.

"Whose side are you on, anyway?" Stephanie demanded.

"Steph, I'm not on *anybody's* side. I'm in the middle . . . and I really and truly hate it."

Stephanie plopped down on the sofa. "Where is my new, agreeable, all-improved self? How could it desert me at a time like this?" She leaned her head back and looked up at the ceiling. "What's gotten into me, Allie? All I can think about is beating Jenni at the talent show. I'm going crazy! I can't eat, I can't sleep, and I'm yelling at my two best friends! Darcy probably won't ever speak to me again."

Allie sat down next to Stephanie and put an arm around her friend's shoulders. "Well," she said, "you *have* been pretty, um, *difficult* lately. Relax! After all, it's only a talent show."

"Only a talent show," Stephanie repeated wearily. "But I just keep thinking that if the Flamingo Dancers win this thing, I'll never be able to walk down the hallway at school and see Jenni Morris's face without wanting to hide in my locker!"

After dinner Stephanie lay on her back on D.J.'s bedroom floor, petting Comet, while her sister tried to study.

"D.J., do you think I'm bossy?" she asked.

"I don't know about that," D.J. said, "but at times you can be a little . . . dictatorial."

"That means bossy, right?" Stephanie said.

"Yeah, I guess it does," D.J. agreed. "But I think it just comes from your wanting everything to go right so badly."

"Oh, I do!" Stephanie agreed earnestly. At least *somebody* understood her.

"Deej," Stephanie asked again. "Do you think our act is good enough to win the talent show?"

"I think you have a great chance at winning," D.J. said.

"Really?" said Stephanie, wanting very much to believe it.

"Really," D.J. said, getting up from her desk and going over to her closet. "Okay, what to wear?" She pulled out a gauzy flower-print dress. "Steve likes this one. I think I'll wear it on our date tonight."

Date made Stephanie think of Ian, and Ian made her think of . . . things she didn't really want to think about. Why in the world had she lied to him? The lie had just made things worse. Now Ian thought she would have gone on a date with him if she didn't have to baby-sit. She had the feeling that before too long, he'd ask her out again. Then what would she say?

"D.J., how do I know if I really like a guy?" she asked.

"Well, it's one of those things you just know," D.J. explained, holding her dress up in front of her and looking into the mirror. "It's like knowing what your favorite flavor of ice cream is. You know without anyone telling you that it's chocolate buttered almond."

Stephanie rolled her eyes. "Why did you have to bring up ice cream at a time like this, D.J.?"

She didn't want to think about Ian asking her out for ice cream!

"Everybody wants me to go out with Ian," Stephanie continued, "even you and Dad, and I don't want to let anybody down—especially Ian. He's asked me out three times, and I don't know what to say. Nobody will let me make up my mind."

"You can't let them make up your mind for you, Steph, that's the important thing. You have to be truthful to yourself—and truthful to him. And I think you really *do* know how you feel, if you'd just listen to yourself."

D.J. waited patiently as Stephanie thought for a while.

"I . . . think I do too," Stephanie said, sitting up straight. "Ian's the kid I grew up with. We shared a sandbox together. I even threw up at his house once. I just don't like him the way you like Steve. He's a totally nice guy, but he's just not chocolate buttered almond."

D.J. laughed and said, "Now you sound more like the Stephanie I know. What took you so long to make up your mind?"

"I guess I was flattered at first," Stephanie admitted. "And then Darcy and Allie wanted me to talk to him about the talent show. But mostly I was afraid to hurt his feelings."

"Comet!" Danny's voice boomed from the doorway. "You're not supposed to be in the girls' bedrooms!"

"But, Dad, he was just lying on the floor," D.J. pointed out as the dog walked sadly out of the room. "He wasn't chewing anything or jumping on the furniture."

"Yes," Danny said, "but he was shedding. I spend a lot of time vacuuming these rooms and—"

"Okay, okay, Dad," D.J. said.

"Oh, by the way, Stephanie," Danny said, "how did your history test go?"

"History test?" Stephanie repeated, stalling for time to think.

"The one you studied all weekend for."

"Oh, *that* history test," Stephanie answered. "Uh, it went. It really went. But we, uh, haven't gotten our grades back yet."

"How do you think you did?" her father asked.

"Oh, you know," Stephanie said slowly, "like usual."

"Great!" Danny put a thumb up. "That's my brilliant daughter. Can't wait for another *A* to hang up on the fridge."

When their father had gone, D.J. looked over at Stephanie. "You flunked, didn't you?" she asked.

"Was it that obvious?" Stephanie asked nervously.

"I don't think Dad noticed," D.J. answered. "He was too busy searching for dog hairs on the rug."

Stephanie sighed. "The truth is, I'm not sure how I did," she said. "I studied a lot, but with all the dance rehearsals and the quarreling, nothing seemed to stay in my head. Oh, D.J., what am I going to do when Dad sees my grade?"

"I don't know," D.J. told her, "but maybe you ought to forget about rehearsing for the talent show and begin rehearsing what you're going to tell him!"

"Tell who what?" came Joey's voice from the doorway.

"Nothing," Stephanie said sadly.

Joey sat down next to Stephanie on the floor and looked at her with concern. "Michelle told me you had some trouble at your rehearsal this afternoon," he said. "Wanna talk about it?"

"Not really," Stephanie muttered.

Joey thought a moment. "Well, then, how about going over to the mall with me?" he suggested. "You look like you could use some cheering up, and I know just the video game that can help!"

Stephanie smiled. Joey always knew exactly what to say.

"Sure!" she said. "Let me get some quarters."

"No, the quarters are on me, Steph," he said, putting a hand on her shoulder. "You look as though you need a treat."

The mall was pretty crowded for a Thursday night, but luckily the video arcade wasn't. In no time Stephanie and Joey went through a whole roll of quarters.

"That made me feel *much* better, Joey," Stephanie said.

"I don't think you're completely cured yet," Joey said, pulling a couple of dollar bills from his wallet. "Here, go get some change and we'll have a few more rounds."

"You're on!" Stephanie ran over to the change machine and fed in the dollars. Humming En Vogue to herself, she waited for the quarters to drop. When they did, she performed a little dance step as she scooped them out.

"Stephanie?" a voice behind her said. "Is that you?"

Startled, Stephanie turned around and found herself face to face with Ian Ezratty. "Ian!" she exclaimed. "Uh . . . hi! What are you doing here?"

"The basketball game ended a half hour ago, and a few of us came over to the Ice Cream Palace," he said. "But I should ask *you* that question. You told me you had to baby-sit tonight."

Stephanie felt her pulse quicken. She'd been caught in a lie! And lying again didn't seem like the way out of it. No, she had to be honest. She'd tell Ian the truth, and now was as good a time as any.

"Ian, I—" she began.

But Ian didn't give her a chance to explain. "Why did you lie to me, Stephanie?" He looked hurt. "If you didn't want to go out with me, you should have just said so."

"I'm really sorry, Ian. See, it's like complicated—"

"Don't bother explaining, Stephanie," Ian interrupted her again. "I don't need to hear any more excuses." And before Stephanie could say another word, he turned and walked away.

Stephanie stood next to the change machine, gripping her fistful of quarters, her mouth still halfway open. She felt terrible. Worse than terrible . . . like she didn't have a friend in the world.

CHAPTER
8

◆ ◀ ▸ ◆

On Friday after third period, Stephanie raced to her locker, where Allie was waiting, impatiently tapping her foot and checking her watch.

"Sorry, Allie," Stephanie panted. "Mr. Elliot kept us after the bell. He went on and on about taste buds and tongues until I was ready to stick mine out at him!" She stopped to catch her breath. "Did you get a chance to talk to Darcy?"

Allie shook her head. "I haven't seen her all day."

"Where could she be?" Stephanie asked. "She didn't meet us at the phone this morning, she wasn't at lunch, and it's practically the end of the day! You think she's absent?"

"No," Allie said. "I know she was in gym class today, because her gym clothes were in our gym locker."

"So what's becoming clear," Stephanie said, leaning against the row of lockers, "is that Darcy's never going to speak to me again. She must really hate me."

"I don't think so, Steph," Allie said. "But if I don't see her by the end of the day, I'll call her at home tonight." She picked up her knapsack. "Listen, I've got to go. There's only a minute and a half to the bell—and my English class is way on the other side of school. Will you be at the bus later?"

"No," Stephanie replied. "D.J. and Steve are picking me up after school today. We promised my dad we'd go to the store and buy dessert."

Allie gasped. "Oh, Steph, tonight's the big Tanner-Ezratty pizza party! What are you going to say to Ian?" Stephanie had told her how she'd run into Ian at the mall, and how she decided she'd apologize to him at dinner.

"I don't know," Stephanie groaned. "Ian isn't

speaking to me either. I tried to talk to him today, but he avoided me. You're the only person I know who's still speaking to me. You *are* still speaking to me, aren't you, Allie?"

"Stephanie, you're overreacting," Allie said. "It'll all work out. You'll see. I'll call you around five, after my piano lesson, okay?"

"Okay," Stephanie said. "Bye."

Stephanie fumbled with the lock on her locker. By the time she got it open and had dumped everything except what she needed for history class, the bell was ringing. *Oh, perfect*, she thought as she slammed shut the locker. Then she took off for the classroom, thankful that all her dancing had gotten her in great shape.

Mr. Spencer was busy talking to a student when Stephanie arrived, so she was able to slip in unnoticed. She took her seat and glanced around. Everyone was looking over the exams!

Stephanie walked up to Mr. Spencer's desk. "Excuse me, Mr. Spencer," she said, "I didn't get my test paper back."

"That's because you weren't here a few minutes ago when I handed them out," Mr. Spencer replied, cocking an eyebrow at her. He reached into his briefcase and took out her graded exam. "Here you are, Miss Tanner."

Stephanie tried to read her teacher's face to tell how she'd done on the test, but his expression didn't give any clues. She took the test from him and, without looking at it, went back to her seat. Then she breathed deeply and looked down at her test. *There's an awful lot of red on here*, she thought. Her eyes moved to the top of the page, and there she saw a big, red *C–*.

It wasn't an *F*. But still, Stephanie's heart sank. Her father was not going to have an *A* to put up on the refrigerator.

"Don't you want your ice cream, Stephanie?" Michelle asked.

Stephanie looked down at the melting chocolate goo in her bowl and shook her head. Ever since she'd lied to Ian, she'd lost her taste for ice cream—even chocolate buttered almond. The Ezrattys—including Ian—had come over for dinner and to watch the game with the Tanners.

"Can D.J. and I split it?" Michelle asked.

Nodding, Stephanie handed Michelle her bowl. She continued chewing on a dry pizza crust and listened to her father, Joey, and Mike yakking away about their good old college days. The six pizza pies had been eaten and Danny had just done all the dishes and was about to start on the kitchen floor when Ian's mother, Helene, had insisted that Danny stop and have some ice cream.

Now the adults were looking at old photo albums and cracking up while the kids watched a video. Stephanie wished she'd gone out to eat Chinese food with Uncle Jesse, Becky, and the twins. Uncle Jesse had insisted that he hated pizza—which everyone knew was his favorite— just so he could avoid another "remember when" session.

When they'd polished off Stephanie's dessert, D.J. and Michelle picked up the ice-cream bowls and headed for the kitchen, leaving Stephanie alone with Ian. She was glad, though—at least now she'd have a chance to explain what she was doing at the video arcade the night before. He'd been avoiding her all evening, and now that they were alone, Stephanie was determined to apologize and patch things up.

"So," she said, trying to start a conversation, "how's it going?"

"Fine," Ian answered flatly, keeping his eyes glued to the TV set.

Stephanie waited for him to ask her how it was going, but he didn't. She persisted. "I heard you won your game last night."

"Yep."

"Did you score many points?"

Ian nodded.

He's making this very hard! Stephanie thought. *But I guess I deserve it.* "So you made the sectionals?" Stephanie asked.

"Uh-huh."

"I bet anything you guys are gonna win state."

Finally Ian spoke. "Uh, Mom?" he called.

"Yes, honey?" Helene Ezratty answered.

"What time is it?"

"It's almost eight," Stephanie piped up before his mother could answer. *At least now he'll have to thank me for giving him the time,* she thought.

But Ian just continued to stare at the TV.

Okay, Stephanie thought. *I'll forget the small talk.* "Listen, Ian," she began, "I have something to tell you."

Just then the doorbell rang, and Ian sprang up

from the couch. He stared toward the door as Joey answered it.

"Come on in," Joey said to whoever it was. "I think we could find a bowl of ice cream for you." But evidently the mysterious caller said no, for Stephanie saw Joey shrug. Then he turned and called, "Ian? Someone's here to see you."

"Right." Ian walked to the door. "Thanks for the pizza, Mr. Tanner," he said as he passed Danny. Then he swung the door wide open and said, "What took you so long?"

Curious, Stephanie got up and went over to the door too. And when she saw who was standing there, her jaw nearly hit the floor. It was Jenni Morris!

Jenni leaned into the living room for a moment. "Hello, everyone!" she said, obviously enjoying herself immensely.

"Jenni?" Stephanie was confused. What was she doing here?

"Ian told me to meet him here," Jenni said, answering Stephanie's unasked question. "We have a date tonight."

"A date?" Stephanie said, unable to do anything but repeat what Jenni had just said.

"Yes, a date," Jenni said sarcastically. "Or maybe you don't know what that is. It's when two people go out to a movie, or a game, or whatever."

"Whatever," Stephanie repeated.

At that moment Ian called good-bye to everyone. D.J. and Michelle came out from the kitchen to say good-bye, and the others said their good-byes from the living room.

"Bye, Stephanie," Ian said over his shoulder. "See ya."

"Yeah," Stephanie managed as she watched Ian and Jenni walk out the door. "See ya."

CHAPTER
9

◆ ◀ ◼ ◆

Stephanie picked up the phone and dialed Allie again. *Oooh!* It was so frustrating to get that annoying busy signal for the twentieth time! Hanging up, Stephanie felt as if she were about to explode from wanting to tell Allie about Ian and Jenni *and* from dying to hear from Allie what Darcy'd had to say.

Since she couldn't get through to Allie, Stephanie trudged back to her room and collapsed on the bed. It was only nine fifteen, and she was incredibly restless. Picking up a magazine, she read the first page, then dropped it to the floor. Absentmindedly, she began throwing her stuffed panda in the air and catching it. She was deep in thought when she heard a knock on her door.

"Steph?" Danny came in and sat next to her on the bed. "So, Ian had a date with someone else tonight."

"Big deal," Stephanie replied.

"Hmmm ... do I detect a bit of jealousy?" Danny asked her.

"I am *not* jealous of Jenni Morris! Besides, Ian doesn't know what he's in for. Jenni is trouble with a capital *T*."

"Well, Ian's a pretty good judge of character," Danny said knowingly. "I'm sure if she's trouble, he'll realize it soon enough. But tell me ... did you ever get your history test back?"

Stephanie thought about saying, "No, not yet," but lying had already gotten her into enough trouble. She nodded. "Today. I don't think you're going to be too happy with my grade."

Danny thought for a moment. "Are *you* happy with your grade?"

"No," Stephanie replied. "I could have done better ... if I'd concentrated better."

"Well, as long as you realize that on your

own," Danny told her, "I have no problem with one low grade. After all, you always bring home excellent grades . . . I'm very proud of you, and I'm sure you'll do better the next time. As far as I'm concerned, this history test is *history!*"

Stephanie smiled. Her father could be so understanding.

Danny was ruffling her hair as D.J. called, "Stephanie, phone! It's Allie!"

Stephanie jumped up, ran into her father's study, and grabbed the phone. "Got it!" she yelled. When she heard D.J. hang up, she plopped down in her father's armchair. "Allie," she said breathlessly. "I've been trying to call you all night."

"I was talking to Darcy, and then my mom had to use the phone before I called you. She was on for like an hour."

"So what'd Darcy say?" Stephanie asked impatiently.

"Nothing too good, Steph," Allie said bleakly. "Darcy's mega-upset. She thinks you're totally out of control."

Stephanie moaned. "She hates me big time?"

"She doesn't hate you," Allie said, "but she's very angry."

Stephanie slumped sideways in the chair and dangled her legs over the arm. "I really blew it this time, didn't I?" she asked sadly. "What should I do, Allie? I don't want to lose Darcy's friendship forever."

"Maybe you should call her and try to talk to her," Allie suggested.

"Do you think she'd talk to me?" Stephanie asked hopefully.

"Yeah," Allie said. "You know Darcy. She can't stay mad at anybody. Maybe if the effort comes from you—if you call and apologize, she'll see that you're really sorry, and you guys can make up."

"Yeah . . ." Stephanie thought for a moment. "You know, she has lacrosse practice on Saturdays. I could go over there tomorrow and apologize to her face to face."

"That'd be great, Stephanie," Allie said.

"Do you want to meet me there? Around noon?" Stephanie asked. "Then, after I talk to Darcy, if . . . everything works out, the three of us can come back here to rehearse."

"Sure," Allie said.

"Perfect," said Stephanie. "Okay, don't hang up. I have some totally major news!"

"What?" Allie asked.

"You are never going to believe who showed up at my front door tonight—to meet Ian for a date!"

"Ian went on a date with someone else?" Allie asked. "Who?"

"Get ready for this . . . Ian is out on a date right this very minute . . . with Jenni Morris!"

There was total silence on the other end. Stephanie waited a moment and then said, "Allie, are you still there? Hello . . ."

"I don't believe it," Allie finally said.

"It is pretty unreal," said Stephanie.

"But . . . but they don't even know each other!" Allie said.

"Apparently they do," Stephanie said. "Boy, Darcy is really going to flip when I tell her." And then, on a serious note, she added, "You know what else this means."

"That Ian has totally lost his mind?" Allie said.

"That," said Stephanie, "but even worse. It looks as though we've lost his vote."

Allie thought for a moment. "I'm not too sure about that. How would Ian ever vote against you? He asked you out."

"Yeah, but I'm not exactly Ian's favorite person these days, even though I'm still going to try to apologize," Stephanie reminded her. "And you know how Jenni is. If there's a sneaky, dishonest way to get Ian's vote . . . she'll find it for sure!"

"So what do we do?" Allie asked. "Just drop out?"

"No way!" Stephanie exclaimed. "We've come too far to drop out now. I mean, if we can get Darcy back—which I'm hoping we can—we might still have a chance. Anyway, I'll see you tomorrow at noon, right?"

"Right."

"If I have to," Stephanie added, before hanging up, "I'll get down on my knees and *beg* for Darcy's forgiveness!"

Slightly before noon, Stephanie peered down the hallway. It always felt weird being in school on a Saturday, as if she were doing something . . . illegal. But although it wasn't a weekday, the school was full of activity. Ms. Zotos was in the office, working on the computer. Basketball practice was under way in the boys' gym, girls were practicing soccer in the west field, and Stephanie heard something with very loud music going on in the girls' gym. Even though she didn't see the lacrosse team, she hoped Darcy was still around somewhere. She'd spoken to Darcy's mother that morning, and Mrs. Powell didn't expect her home until after one.

At noon on the dot, Allie's mom dropped her off in front of the school. Stephanie waved her inside. "Hurry, Allie!" she called. "I think lacrosse practice is already over."

"Maybe Darcy's in the locker room, changing," suggested Allie. "Let's go down and check."

The two walked toward the girls' gym to go down the stairs to the locker room. As they neared the gym, the music coming from inside grew louder and louder. "I hear Janet Jackson," Stephanie said as she pushed open the heavy gym doors. "What's going on in here?"

Allie entered the gym first and stopped short. "Oh, my gosh!" she exclaimed in horror.

Stephanie crowded into the doorway beside Allie. In an instant, it was clear to her what all the music and commotion were about—Jenni Morris and the Flamingo Dancers were rehearsing their act for the talent show. But that wasn't what had reduced Allie and then Stephanie to shock victims. Dancing right along with all the Flamingoes was none other than Darcy Powell!

Before Stephanie or Allie could say a word, Jenni spotted them in the doorway.

"Stephanie Tanner and Allie Taylor! Well, well, well. Have you spies come to steal the Hip Hoppers' best moves?" she asked, snapping off the music.

Stephanie and Allie exchanged looks. "The *Hip Hoppers*?" Stephanie asked.

"Right!" Jenni grinned. "Don't you love our act's new name? I just went into the office ten minutes ago and registered it with Ms. Zotos, so it's official."

Stephanie could have kicked herself for not remembering to go back to the office last week and write down the Hip Hop Girls. Now it was too late. They'd lost their name and . . . Darcy! There she was, standing between two eighth graders.

But Darcy wasn't looking at her. She was looking at the floor, nervously shifting back and forth.

"Oh, and I can't thank you enough for being so creepy that Darcy quit your group," Jenni said. "It's great for us! She's the best!"

Stephanie couldn't believe it. "Darcy, is this true?" she asked. "Are you dancing with them now?"

Darcy couldn't seem to bring herself to look Stephanie or Allie in the eye. "Um . . . well . . . I . . ." she stammered.

Stephanie didn't wait to hear more. It was obvious that Darcy *was* part of Jenni's act now. Grabbing hold of Allie's arm, Stephanie yanked her out of the gym, letting the doors slam behind them.

"That traitor!" Stephanie cried, pacing the hallway furiously.

"I can't believe Darcy would do something like this!" Allie said, shaking her head. "It's not like her. I just can't believe it. Think we should try and talk to her or something?"

"Talk to her? What for?" Stephanie replied angrily. "She's made up her mind. She'd rather dance with Jenni than with us!"

"Maybe there's some . . . good explanation," Allie offered.

"Like what?" Stephanie asked.

Allie could only shrug.

"She must be doing this to get back at me," Stephanie said. "Fine! If she wants to dance with Jenni, then let her. We'll see who has the last laugh after we beat them at the talent show!"

"What are you talking about, Stephanie? How can we possibly enter the talent show *now*? Without Darcy, we don't have an act."

"Sure we do!" Stephanie insisted.

"How?" Allie asked. "All our moves are for *three* dancers."

"So? I can fix that."

"There's no time to rechoreograph everything and learn new moves," Allie went on frantically. "I can't do it . . . not with the talent show just a week away! Face it. Without Darcy, we don't stand a chance."

"Listen to me, Allie," Stephanie said. "First of all, we *can* get by with only two dancers. I know all the moves, and I'll help you with your part."

Allie put her head in her hands. "It'll never work."

"I know what I'm talking about," Stephanie insisted. "The dancing part's no problem. It's the judges we have to worry about. What if I have a little private chat with Debra Mostow? Once I tell her all about the *real* Jenni, about how sneaky and dishonest she and the Flamingoes are, Debra definitely won't want to be Jenni's friend anymore! That's where you come in."

"*Me?*" Allie asked. "I don't know ..."

"Just go up to Debra in the hallway and be all nice to her and maybe invite her to your house for dinner or something, then the next night, I'll invite her to my house, and ..."

"You've totally lost it, Stephanie."

"We'll be such good friends with Debra by showtime on Friday night, she'll have forgotten all about the Flamingoes! And the first prize will be ours!"

Allie tried to speak, but Stephanie couldn't be stopped.

"Wait! I've got an even better idea!" Stephanie said excitedly. "Why don't we try and get Darah Judson on our side too? But ... that's a tough one, her being a Flamingo and all."

"Stephanie Tanner?" Allie called. "Hello? Earth to Stephanie . . ."

Stephanie snapped her fingers. "Wait! Even better! We'll get her out of the way. Listen, on the night of the talent show, I'll call Darah's house and tell her there's a delivery of flowers for her. I'll say they're from a secret admirer and that she has to be home to sign for them. Then she'll miss the show, and . . ."

Suddenly Allie reached out and clamped her hand over Stephanie's mouth.

"MMmmpphhh!" Stephanie tried to speak.

"Not a chance," Allie said, taking control of the situation. "Now you listen to me, Stephanie Tanner. Calm down and take a minute and think about what you've been saying and how utterly and completely wacko you sound! Then maybe . . . just maybe, I'll think about removing my hand."

"MMMmmpphh! HHHmmpphh!" Stephanie pleaded.

"Will you be good?" Allie asked.

Stephanie nodded.

"Okay," Allie said, "but no funny stuff. No plotting or planning or crazy ideas or anything!" Slowly she removed her hand.

Stephanie cleared her throat and took a big breath. "I'm okay now. Thanks, Allie. I don't know what got into me."

"That's better," Allie said. "Now let's get out of here."

As they walked toward the Tanner house, Stephanie could feel Allie staring at her strangely.

"What?" Stephanie asked impatiently.

"Stephanie," Allie said. "That was scary. You were starting to act just like a Flamingo. Just like Jenni Morris!"

CHAPTER
10

♦ ◂ ◾ ♦

"Oh, come on," said D.J. as she sat on Stephanie's bed, brushing Michelle's hair. "Darcy couldn't be that stupid."

"It's true!" Stephanie insisted. "Right, Allie?"

Allie nodded. "But I still think there must be some reasonable explanation for it," she said. "I mean, Darcy *hates* Jenni. Why would she become so friendly with her all of a sudden?"

"Well, you saw her with your own eyes!" Stephanie reminded Allie. "She was dancing around the gym with Jenni Morris."

"Who is Jenni Morris?" Michelle asked innocently.

"She's this monster we go to school with," said Stephanie.

Michelle's eyes widened. "Why would Darcy want to dance with a monster?"

"My point exactly!" Allie said. "There must be something we don't know about . . ."

"Get a clue, Allie!" Stephanie said. "There *isn't* any reasonable explanation. Darcy was so mad about the Hip Hop Girls costumes that she decided to go over to the other side. And since she did that, we'll just have to fight fire with fire. We'll rework our entire routine and make it three hundred percent better than before! We'll make it so amazing, we'll be the envy of every Flamingo in school!"

"I hope I can do it, Steph," Allie said. "You know I can't dance the way you can."

"You'll be great, Allie. Don't worry." Stephanie looked over to her sisters. "D.J., Michelle, want to come watch us rehearse?"

"Not today," D.J. said, putting down the hairbrush. "Steve and I are going to the mall to buy sneakers."

"What about you, Michelle?"

"Can I dance Darcy's part?" Michelle asked for the billionth time.

"Michelle, there *is* no Darcy's part anymore!" Stephanie explained. "It's just a twosome now—me and Allie!"

"Then no thanks," Michelle said. "I'll go with D.J. and Steve." On her way out the door she turned. "Stephanie, you're coming to my dance recital on Tuesday, right?"

"Dance recital?" Stephanie asked.

Michelle rolled her eyes. "Yes! I told you a week ago! It's Tuesday night, and I have the best part. You have to come!"

Stephanie smiled at her little sister. "I'll definitely be there. Don't worry, you can count on me."

"You really ought to see Michelle's solo," D.J. said, getting up to leave. "She's spent a lot of time working on it, and it's a show stealer!"

After D.J. and Michelle left, Stephanie and Allie quickly changed into their workout clothes and ran downstairs to set up the living room for their rehearsal.

"Wow, this couch seems heavy today," Stephanie said as they tried to shove it out of the way.

"That's because Darcy usually moves it with us," Allie pointed out.

"Yeah, I guess." Slowly Stephanie walked over to the boom box, but instead of turning it on, she just stood next to it.

"What's wrong?" Allie asked. "You haven't said a word for a whole thirty seconds."

"I think you're right—there is a good explanation for why Darcy was dancing with Jenni," said Stephanie softly. "It's me! I'm the reason she quit our group and went over to theirs. I drove her away!"

"That's what I tried to tell you," Allie said. "You were acting so *weird*, it was hard to tell what you were going to do from one moment to the next!"

Stephanie sat down on the sofa. "What's with me, anyway?"

"You went talent-show crazy!" Allie said, making Stephanie smile a little. "At first, when we heard about the show," Allie went on, "it was going to be this totally fun thing the three of us were planning. Then *boom!* Along came Jenni Morris, and when you found out she was involved, it was like, good-bye, Sane Stephanie, hello, Stephanie's Competition-Crazed Evil Twin!"

Stephanie groaned and put her head down on the crook of her arm. "I've been *that* bad?"

"Let's just say," Allie replied, "that you came this close to winning the Obnoxiousness Award this afternoon when you suggested sending flowers to Darah Judson's house!"

Stephanie laughed. "I *did* say that, didn't I?"

"Boy," Allie said, "were you on a roll!"

Stephanie jumped up. "Okay, I'm really and truly through being obnoxious and bossy. If Darcy will only forgive me, I promise never to tell anyone what to do again for as long as I live!" As she finished this declaration, the door-bell rang.

Stephanie opened the door and gasped. "Darcy!"

Darcy stood in the doorway, now looking directly at Stephanie with red, puffy eyes. "Can I come in?" She sniffed.

"Of course you can!" Stephanie said. "What happened to you?"

When she saw Darcy's sorry state, Allie put an arm around her and led her to the couch. "Darcy, what's the matter?"

Darcy tried to get the words out but ended

up sobbing. Between her tears and her sniffling, Stephanie and Allie couldn't make out a thing she was saying except something about Jenni Morris and something about a sprained ankle.

"Darce," Stephanie said, "come into the kitchen."

"Okay," Darcy agreed between sobs.

Darcy and Allie sat at the counter while Stephanie served them each a glass of juice and a slice of carrot cake. They sipped quietly for a moment, giving Darcy a chance to calm down.

At last Darcy looked at her friends. "You must hate me," she said.

"Not me!" Stephanie piped up.

Darcy took a deep breath. "Okay, here goes," she said. "I got to school early this morning for lacrosse practice, so I went inside the building, and I heard music coming from the gym. I poked my head in—just like you guys did—and saw Jenni and her friends rehearsing. I watched for a second, then Jenni spotted me and accused me of spying for you, Steph. So I . . . I told her I wasn't dancing with you guys anymore."

Darcy stopped to blow her nose and catch her

breath. She managed to take a bite of cake and a sip of juice, too.

"Anyway," she continued, "you should have seen her, Steph. The minute she heard I'd quit the group, she put on that phony 'you-can-talk-to-your-best-friend-Jenni' routine, and right then, I . . . I sort of needed a friend."

Stephanie nodded. "Yeah, I've fallen for that act, too. But I know now that Jenni Morris is *never* a friend."

"You can say that again!" Darcy said. "Anyway, the next thing I know, she's telling me that one of their lead dancers twisted her ankle and that they had an opening in their act. She practically begged me to join!

"I was still so mad at you, Stephanie," Darcy confessed. "Jenni made it sound as if I was going to be their lead dancer or something, and all I could think about was getting back at you and making you jealous. I knew dancing with Jenni would do the trick. That's why I did it." A new round of tears welled up in Darcy's eyes. "I'm sorry, Steph."

"That's okay, Darcy," Stephanie said warmly.

"Actually, I feel better knowing I'm not the only one with an evil twin."

"Huh?" said Darcy.

"Never mind," Stephanie said. "I'm really sorry about the way I've been acting lately."

"Anyway," Darcy went on, "after lacrosse practice I went back and started rehearsing with Jenni, and she asked my opinion about things, put me up in the front row of dancers . . . she even told me I was an excellent dancer, so when she asked me what name you guys had chosen for your act, I just told her. I never thought she'd steal it! Believe me, I was just as surprised as you were when she said they were the Hip Hoppers."

"That thief!" Stephanie said.

"So then," Darcy said, "you guys showed up." She stopped for a second because the tears were beginning again. "I felt really bad when I saw you guys . . . I didn't know what to say, and then you left so quickly—"

"We wanted to go back and talk to you," Allie interrupted, "but we weren't sure what was going on."

"After you left," Darcy said, "that's when

Jenni asked me to show her our En Vogue routine. I did a little of it for her, but I felt guilty and stopped. The next thing I know, Jenni's saying how I should move back a row, then she cut my solo. By the time the rehearsal was over, I was practically *scenery*! And when I got home, she called me up."

"Who, Jenni?" Stephanie asked with a mouthful of cake.

Darcy nodded. "She said her friend's ankle was all better and that they didn't need me in the act after all!"

"Jenni Morris strikes again!" said Stephanie angrily.

"Really," Darcy agreed. "And I don't think I was the only one who was burned by Jenni today."

"What do you mean?" Stephanie asked.

"Debra Mostow showed up at the gym," Darcy explained. "She looked really excited about something, and she went over to talk to Jenni. But Jenni started screaming at her and told her to get out. Debra looked pretty upset when she left."

Stephanie and Allie exchanged looks. "I wonder what that was all about," Stephanie said.

"Who knows?" Darcy said, shrugging.

"But even if Debra doesn't vote for the Hip Hoppers, Jenni's still got Ian and Darah Judson on her side," Stephanie pointed out. "That's two judges out of three."

"Jenni and the Hip Hoppers are pretty good dancers," said Darcy, "but our choreography is a zillion times better. If the judging is at all fair, I think we stand a pretty good chance."

"*We?*" Stephanie asked, smiling. "Does that mean you're back in the group, Darcy?"

"If you'll have me," Darcy said shyly.

Stephanie beamed. "Of course we will!" she said, breathing a sigh of relief. "I thought you wouldn't want to come back because of me! I know I've been worse than Jenni Morris lately. But I promise—no more bossiness, no more dishing out orders."

"And I won't complain so much," Darcy said.

The girls hugged, then looked over at Allie.

"What?" Allie asked. "What are you looking at me for? *I* won't be bossy or complain, okay?"

Stephanie and Darcy laughed.

107

"You deserve a medal for trying so hard to keep the peace!" Stephanie said, giving Allie a hug. "If it hadn't been for you, we'd have broken up before becoming big and famous! But now, thanks to you, Allie, we'll be dancing on MTV in no time!"

CHAPTER
11

◆ ◣ ◆ ◆

After school on Tuesday, Stephanie, Allie, and Darcy flew past Jesse and Becky, who were in the living room watching "Sesame Street" with the twins, and raced up the stairs. Stephanie and Allie flung their book bags on the floor and made themselves comfortable on Stephanie's bed while Darcy got ready for the big costume unveiling.

Darcy had been working on her costume in secret for three whole days, and the girls were positively dying of curiosity.

"You're gonna flip when you see it!" Darcy said excitedly. "I hate to brag, but boy, am I good!"

"Okay, okay!" Allie cried. "Let's see it already!"

Dramatically, Darcy reached into her big canvas bag and pulled out a costume. "Ta-da!" she said, holding it up.

The girls' eyes sparkled when they saw what Darcy had done. She'd taken the plain, black outfit Stephanie had originally thought of and, by adding patterns of colorful beadwork in ever-widening swirls starting at the neckline and looping wildly around the whole bodysuit, she'd turned it into something absolutely incredible.

Stephanie stood up, her eyes wide with amazement. "Wow!" she said breathlessly. "Darcy, this is beautiful!"

Allie took the bodysuit from Stephanie. "Darcy, you made this yourself?"

"Yup!" Darcy said proudly.

"Wow," both Stephanie and Allie said again.

"Does this mean you approve?" Darcy asked.

Stephanie laughed. "I think you could say that! Where'd you learn how to do this?" she asked, impressed by the amount of work Darcy had put into the costume. Stephanie ran her fingers delicately over the beading. "It's so . . . *cool!* Just the right amount of color and flash."

"Wait!" said Darcy. "There's more!" Reaching again into her bag, she pulled out a pair of black canvas sneakers. Not only were the laces decorated with the same iridescent beads, but Darcy had also superglued beads in a pattern that went all around the ankles. The whole outfit matched perfectly.

"Truly excellent!" Stephanie proclaimed.

Darcy bowed playfully. "Thank you, thank you," she said. "Once I came up with the pattern, the rest was easy. Steph, give me your bodysuit and shorts before I leave today and I'll start on your costume tonight. Allie, bring me your stuff tomorrow night when you come to my house for rehearsal."

As Stephanie rummaged through her closet, looking for her black leotard and biker shorts, Allie said, "By the way, what's going on with you and Ian?"

Stephanie tossed Darcy her outfit and sighed. "I left four messages for him at home, but he hasn't called me back. And I didn't see him in school yesterday or today, either. I think our friendship is history."

"I still can't believe you didn't want to go out with him," Darcy said.

Stephanie groaned. "Let's not start that again!"

"Okay, okay!" Darcy said. "I'm just saying it."

Stephanie put her head back in the closet to look for her black sneakers. "Here they are!" she said finally, handing them over to Darcy.

"So, we're one hundred percent ready now, huh?" Darcy asked.

Stephanie sighed. "Except for the intro. It's crazy, but our entire routine seems so fabulous, I'm stuck on the intro because it's got to be so totally, amazingly perfect."

"We also need a new name for our act," Darcy reminded them.

"How about the Elvis Presley Dancers?" Uncle Jesse suggested, coming into Stephanie's room with Nicky on his back.

The girls groaned.

"Jesse, don't be silly," said Becky, who came in behind him with Alex. "The girls need a cool, trendy name. Like . . . like the Cools or the Trends. Or hey, what about the Cool Trends?"

"Well, that's certainly, um, cool and trendy," Stephanie said, rolling her eyes so only Allie and Darcy could see.

At that moment D.J. called up to them, "Let's go, guys!"

"Oops!" Jesse said. "Almost forgot why we came up, Steph. It's time to leave for Michelle's recital. Your father and Joey have already gone."

Stephanie slapped her forehead. "Michelle's dance recital! I completely forgot! Sorry, guys," she said to Darcy and Allie. "I gotta go. We'll vote on a new name tomorrow at lunch, okay?"

"No problem," Allie said.

"Come on, Allie," Darcy said. "Walk me to my house. Maybe we'll think of a new name on the way."

"Okay. Bye, Steph," Allie said. "Wish Michelle good luck from me!"

"From me, too!" Darcy said. "We'll see ya tomorrow."

At the recital hall, the Tanner party took up nearly two whole rows. Stephanie got comfortable in her aisle seat and opened her program.

"All I've heard for a week now is how great

Michelle's solo is," Stephanie said to D.J. "Her class is dancing to *Swan Lake*—what part does she have?"

"Just wait," said D.J. "You'll see."

Waiting for the program to begin, Stephanie looked around the auditorium and was surprised to see Debra Mostow a few rows in front of her. *What is she doing here?* Stephanie wondered. *Who has she come to see?*

"Who are you staring at?" D.J. asked her.

"Oh, uh . . . Debra Mostow," Stephanie answered. "She's in my class and . . . she's one of the judges in the talent show. Maybe I should go over and say hello . . ."

"I thought Allie made you promise to stop scheming," said D.J. slyly.

"Scheming?" Stephanie was insulted. "I just want to say hello and be friendly, that's all." *And maybe find out what the big fight Debra had with Jenni was all about*, she thought.

Stephanie got up and walked across the aisle and down a few rows. "Debra?" she said.

Debra turned in her seat. At first, Stephanie could tell she didn't recognize her, but after a second or so a smile came across her face. "Oh, hi!" she said. "Stephanie . . . right?"

Stephanie smiled back. "Right."

Debra motioned to the empty seat next to her. "You want to sit?" she asked.

"Sure," Stephanie said, taking the seat. "So, let me guess . . . You have a little sister in the show?"

Debra laughed and nodded.

"Me too!" Stephanie said. "Mine's in Miss Black's class."

"My sister has Miss Black too," said Debra. "Our sisters are probably in the same number!" She checked the program. "What's your sister's name?"

"Michelle Tanner," Stephanie said.

Debra looked up. "Michelle Tanner is your sister? My sister told me she has the lead tonight."

"I guess I've been so busy getting ready for *our* dance number, you know, for the talent show, that I haven't had a chance to see Michelle's routine yet."

"How's your act coming along?" Debra asked.

"Really great," Stephanie said, smiling. "My friends Allie and Darcy and I have been rehearsing every spare moment. We're ready." Except for the intro, but she was hardly going to tell *that* to one of the judges!

"Well, all I can say," Debra said, "is that I hope you guys beat Jenni Morris and the dumb Hip Hoppers!"

"But I thought you were friends with Jenni," said Stephanie.

"I was," Debra replied. "Or at least I *thought* I was. But once Jenni learned I'd resigned from being a judge for the show, she dropped me like a hot potato!"

Stephanie leaned back in her seat. "Yup, that sounds like the Jenni Morris I know!" she said.

"You know her pretty well?" Debra asked.

"Someday I'll tell you all about it," Stephanie said. "But what happened? How come you're not going to be a judge?"

"I wanted to be *in* the show," Debra explained. "That's why I went to the principal's office and resigned as a judge. Jenni was always complaining about all the problems she was having with the choreography, so I thought it would be fun to surprise her and join her group. I've been taking dance lessons since I was four years old," she added, "so I know a little bit about putting together a dance routine.

"Anyway," she went on, "when Jenni heard I'd resigned, she flipped and kicked me out of the Flamingoes. Obviously she was only using me for my vote."

"I'm sorry if she upset you," said Stephanie. "She has that effect on people." As the lights dimmed in the auditorium, Stephanie whispered, "Did you say you've been dancing since you were four?"

Debra nodded. "Ballet, jazz, tap . . . you name it and I've danced it! When we lived in Florida, I even learned how to square dance."

"So," Stephanie said. "You can probably pick up a new routine pretty fast, right?"

Debra snapped her fingers in answer.

"Listen," said Stephanie, "I have an excellent idea. Would you like to dance with *us* in the talent show?"

Debra's face broke into a huge smile. "That would be awesome! But are you sure your friends wouldn't mind?"

"No way," Stephanie assured her.

"Then I'd love to," Debra said happily.

Before they could say another word, the lights in the hall went down all the way and the music to *Swan Lake* came on. Stephanie and Debra settled into their seats to watch the show.

"Ladies and gentlemen," a voice announced in the dark, "welcome to the Twelfth Annual Bay Area Little Dance Company Recital. I would like to introduce tonight's emcee, one of our star dancers . . . Michelle Tanner!"

Stephanie's eyes widened. She was surprised at the grand introduction, and even more surprised at the loud cheering from the audience in her little sister's honor. Then she remembered that half the audience was made up of her family.

Suddenly a spotlight flickered on, and there was Michelle onstage, all by herself. People started to laugh when they saw her, dressed in a tuxedo and top hat and holding a cane. This was not what anyone expected to see in *Swan Lake*—which was a ballet!

Debra leaned over to Stephanie. "She looks soooo adorable!"

Michelle flipped her top hat up and caught it. Then she began to dance to *Swan Lake*. But the funny part was, she was *tap* dancing! Then the spotlight followed her across the stage, where she was joined one by one by her classmates, who were all wearing tutus! The audience went nuts! Even Stephanie couldn't help but laugh. She'd never seen anyone tap-dance the *Swan Lake* ballet in a tuxedo and top hat.

Click! A lightbulb suddenly went on in Stephanie's head. "Omigosh!" she said, grabbing hold of the arms on her chair. "I've got it!"

"Got what?" Debra asked.

"The perfect introduction!"

CHAPTER
12

◆ ◢ ◣ ◆

Stephanie stood looking at her reflection in the full-length mirror backstage at the school auditorium. Behind her, kids were pushing and shoving as they tried to get a peek at themselves.

"Hurry up!" someone called out. "Stop hogging the mirror!"

"Chill out!" she replied. "I'll be finished in a second."

Taking her time, she adjusted the shoulders of her leotard and checked her costume overall. She liked what she saw.

When she was satisfied that she looked spectacular, Stephanie skipped over to where Allie,

Darcy, and Debra were waiting by the exit sign in the hallway. Their group had been assigned to wait there, along with the other singing and dancing acts, for their turn to perform. Stephanie double-checked the lineup that was posted on the wall by the fire emergency exit. Their act was to go on second to last, right before the finale. The night before they'd all voted on a name for the group. It had been a unanimous vote for Debra's suggestion: the Groove Girls.

"We have a long wait," Stephanie said to her friends, "but obviously they're saving the best for last!"

"This is so exciting!" said Debra, smiling and looking around at all the hoopla. "I'm really glad you guys let me dance with you."

"Hey, we're the ones who are glad," Darcy said cheerfully. "You're as great a dancer as I am a costume designer."

"Such modesty." Stephanie looked again down the hallway. "No one's seen Jenni and the Hip Hoppers yet?"

"Not yet," Darcy said.

"Maybe they're not coming!" Allie said hopefully.

"Maybe they found out how great we are," Debra offered, "and they chickened out!"

The other girls laughed.

"Even if they haven't heard how great we are," Stephanie said, "they'll find out what they're up against soon enough!"

"Hey, is anybody else a little ... *nervous*?" Allie asked.

"Are you kidding?" said Debra. "I'm shaking in my sneakers! No matter how many times I dance in front of people, I always get butterflies in my stomach."

"Me too," Stephanie confessed. "But not butterflies ... more like *bats*!"

"It's safe to say we're *all* freaked out!" Darcy exclaimed.

"That's good," Allie said. "I'd hate to be the only one."

Darcy leaned over to Stephanie. "So where's our little 'secret weapon'?" she whispered.

Stephanie smiled mischievously. "Don't worry, Darce. Our secret weapon—"

"Shhh!" said Allie suddenly. "Keep it secret! Look who's here!"

All four turned to see Jenni and two other Flamingoes coming into the hallway wearing white T-shirts and red satin shorts.

"*Those* are their hot costumes?" Stephanie said.

"They look more like cheerleaders than dancers," said Debra.

Darcy laughed, covering her mouth. "Can these three be all that's left of the Hip Hoppers?" she said in amazement. "Last Saturday they had *eight* dancers!"

"They probably all got tired of being bossed around by Jenni, so they dropped out," Stephanie said cheerfully. And then added, "And you *know* how everyone hates to be bossed around."

"Really!" agreed Allie and Darcy together.

Jenni and her friends strolled down the hallway, trying to look like they didn't have a care in the world. When she saw Stephanie and the others, Jenni immediately put on one of her famous phony smiles. But as she took in their costumes, her smile quickly faded.

"What are *you* doing with *them*?" Jenni asked Debra.

"They asked me to dance with them," Debra

said. "And I said yes because I wanted to dance with *winners*."

"Oh, puh-lease!" Jenni scowled, then looked at Darcy. "I thought they kicked you out," she said obnoxiously.

Darcy folded her arms across her chest. "Well, Jenni, you thought wrong."

Jenni's face turned red. Turning to her friends, she said, "Let's get out of here."

"Did you see the look on Jenni's face when she saw our outfits?" Stephanie asked.

"I, for one, will never forget it!" Darcy said.

"But now let's forget all about Jenni and her no-talent nondancers," said Stephanie. "Let's go out there and have a great time! What do you say?"

Allie smiled. "I'm with you, Stephanie."

"That goes for me too!" Darcy added happily.

"Count me in!" Debra said.

"Whether we win or lose this thing tonight," proclaimed Stephanie, "long live the Groove Girls!"

At last, after they had waited in the wings through everyone else's act, it was finally time for Stephanie, Allie, Darcy, and Debra to take their places on center stage. In the dim light they got into their starting positions behind the curtain. Stephanie looked over to stage left and signaled their "secret weapon" to wait.

The curtain went up, and the girls remained frozen in position in the dark. When the music started, everyone expected the lights to come on, but only one did—a little spotlight. And it was way over on stage left ... on secret-weapon Michelle!

As soon as the audience saw her—looking like a little darling in her tuxedo and top hat—dozens of "oohs" and "ahhs" came from the crowd. Even Stephanie and the other dancers had a hard time trying not to smile.

Right on cue, Michelle picked up a big, sparkling sign and held it in front of her. It read: THE GROOVE GIRLS. Then, to the beat of the music, Michelle tapped across the stage, directly in front of Stephanie and the others, all the while wiggling the sign in front of her. The audience cracked up! When Michelle reached the opposite end of the stage, she flipped the sign over and showed it to the audience. It read: WHAT AN

INTRO! And the audience cracked up a second time.

As the Groove Girls began their dance routine, the audience was already loving it. Everybody cheered and clapped to the beat, and each time the girls performed an impressive move, the cheering grew even louder! When at last the routine ended, the applause took a full two minutes to die down.

The girls rushed off the stage and fell into a big bear hug, jumping up and down and squealing.

"We were great!" Stephanie yelled.

"Better than great!" Darcy bellowed.

"The best!" Debra said breathlessly.

"Why was I so nervous?" Allie said. "That was a breeze!"

Stephanie burst out laughing, she was so relieved. "You had nothing to worry about. It was me I was worried about!"

"You?" Allie said, amazed. "But you're the best dancer of us all!"

"Hey, where's Michelle?" Stephanie asked.

"Yeah!" Darcy said. "I want to congratulate our little secret weapon!"

"I'm right here," said Michelle from over by

the curtain, where she was watching the last act. "Was I okay?"

"Michelle, you were awesome!" Allie said. "You brought down the house!"

"Talk about a snazzy intro!" Darcy gushed. "It was genius!"

Michelle wore an enormous smile. "Thanks!" she said.

"Hold it! Listen!" Stephanie said, quieting them down. "They're about to announce the winner!"

The girls scampered over to the side of the stage, where all the other performers were already waiting to hear the results.

The principal, Mr. Thomas, was onstage, smiling and holding up two trophies. "We have a tie for first place!" he said into the microphone. The audience fell silent.

The principal cleared his throat and continued. "The winners are—Susan Gedal for her hilarious stand-up comedy routine, and the Groove Girls for their dance number!"

"Aaaahhhhhh!" Stephanie screamed, and jumped up and down. She grabbed hold of her friends and her sister, and soon the five of them were screaming and jumping again.

"Go on, guys!" someone near Stephanie said, and before she quite knew what was happening, she and the other Groove Girls were being pushed through the crowd onto the stage.

The foursome and Michelle took the stage holding hands and walked over to Mr. Thomas to get their trophy. Stephanie looked out and saw her family in the first two rows, giving them a standing ovation. She smiled and waved.

Mr. Thomas handed Stephanie their trophy and offered his congratulations. After saying thank you, Stephanie turned and gave the trophy to Michelle, and the audience cheered even louder. Then the girls skipped off the stage.

Backstage, they were all inspecting their award when somebody tapped Stephanie on the shoulder.

Stephanie spun around, half-expecting to see her father. But it wasn't her dad—it was Ian Ezratty.

"Ian!" she said, truly glad to see him. "Hi!"

"You guys were great, Stephanie!" Ian said. "You got all the judges' votes."

Stephanie smiled. "Thanks," she said. "But I'm a little surprised. I thought for sure you'd vote for Jenni."

"Why would you think that?" Ian asked, looking confused.

"Well, because you two are dating and—"

"Stephanie," Ian said, stopping her, "first of all, I'd never do that—vote for Jenni just because we were dating. And second . . . we're *not* dating!"

"Oh, really?" said Stephanie. "Then who was that at my front door the other night?"

"That was Jenni," Ian said, looking sheepish. "Listen, I knew that she was only interested in me because I was a judge for the show, but when she asked me out for Friday, I agreed to go because . . . because . . ."

"Because why?" Stephanie asked.

Ian shrugged. "If she was using me because she thought she could get my vote, then I thought I could use her to make you jealous," he answered. "When I saw you at the mall after my game and realized that you'd lied about having to baby-sit, I was pretty bummed out."

Stephanie bit her bottom lip. Now—right

now—was the perfect opportunity to come clean and tell Ian the truth, and she had to do it. There'd be no more lying for her!

"Listen, Ian," she began, "I'm really sorry I lied to you. I just didn't know how to tell you how I felt."

"How *do* you feel?" Ian asked.

Stephanie took a deep breath. "You know I like you, Ian," she said. "But as a friend. A very good, very close friend," she added, "but a friend. I didn't want things to be any different between us from the way they've always been, but I didn't know how to say no to the date, so I made up that excuse about having to baby-sit."

To her surprise, Ian smiled. "Stephanie, you can date anyone you want. And if you just want to be friends with me, that's totally cool. I thought you hated me or something. I'd rather be your friend than nothing at all!"

Stephanie felt so relieved. "Thanks, Ian," she said. "And I mean it . . . I'm really sorry about lying to you."

"Hey! There she is!" Danny's voice rang out. "My talented dancing daughter!"

Danny Tanner came flying backstage, followed by Joey, D.J., Uncle Jesse, Aunt Becky, and the twins. Danny picked Stephanie up in his arms and twirled her around. "You were terrific, sweetheart!" he said with a huge, proud grin. "I knew you'd win!"

"Thanks, Dad!" Stephanie said.

"Nice going, Steph!" said Joey.

"Congratulations, Stephanie!" Uncle Jesse said, winking.

"Thank you, thank you very much," Stephanie said in her best Elvis Presley voice.

Jesse and Becky laughed.

"Hey! What about me?" Michelle asked, tugging at her father's shirt.

"Michelle," Danny said, picking up his smallest daughter. "You were fantastic too!" He gave her a hug and a kiss. "The best intro I've ever seen!"

Darcy, Debra, and Allie's families were all crowding backstage, and congratulations were flying.

"Hey!" Danny said above the noise. "What do you all say to taking the Groove Girls out to celebrate?"

Everyone seemed to approve of this suggestion. Danny turned to his middle daughter. "So, Steph, where's it going to be? Can you think of someplace big enough to take us all?"

Stephanie put her finger to her chin. "Hmm . . ." she said. "Well, the mall's pretty big," she said. "How do we all feel about going to the Ice Cream Palace?"

Michelle was the first to agree, and the loudest.

"To the mall!" shouted Joey, rounding up some passengers for his car.

"We'll meet you there," said Allie's mother.

Debra's father nodded his agreement.

As the crowd thinned, Stephanie turned to Ian. "Come with us, okay, Ian?" Now that they understood each other, she thought it would be great to have Ian come along.

"Are you sure you want me to?" Ian asked.

"Positive," Stephanie replied. "And with about thirty-five people going with us, I don't think anybody would call it a date."

Ian laughed. "Well, if I'd known you felt this way," he said, "I could have asked the whole basketball team to come with us on Thursday night."

Stephanie laughed as they raced for the parking lot. Now that things were all right with Ian, Stephanie realized she was hungry! She was definitely ready to eat ice cream again—and lots of it.